Lowcountry Voodoo

UNITED STATES
THE GULLAH
ST. HELENA ISLAND
CHARLESTON
JOHNS ISLAND
SAPELO ISLAND
BEAUFORT
SAVANNAH

N

W E

S

AFRICA

Lowcountry

VOODOO

Beginner's Guide to Tales, Spells and Boo Hags

Terrance Zepke

Illustrations by Michael Swing

Pineapple Press, Inc.
Sarasota, Florida

Inquiries should be addressed to:

Pineapple Press, Inc.
P.O. Box 3889
Sarasota, Florida 34230

www.pineapplepress.com

Library of Congress Cataloging-in-Publication Data

Zepke, Terrance
  Lowcountry voodoo : beginner's guide to tales, spells, and boo hags / Terrance Zepke. -- 1st ed.
      p. cm.
  Includes bibliographical references and index.
  ISBN 978-1-56164-455-1 (pb : alk. paper)
  1. Voodooism--South Carolina. 2. Voodooism--Georgia. 3. South Carolina--Religion. 4. Georgia--Religion. I. Title.
  BL2490.Z47 2009
  299.6'7509757--dc22
                                                    2009030608

First Edition
10 9 8 7 6 5 4 3 2

Design by Shé Hicks
Printed in the United States of America

Be advised: The practices described in this book are given only for their historic and cultural significance. We are not suggesting readers should even attempt to cast spells or make charms and voodoo dolls. We advise against leaving burning candles unsupervised or having loaded firearms accessible in the home. We are not recommending use of the herbs and other ingredients for the various potions and remedies mentioned in this book. The publisher and author disclaim liability for any claim brought as the result of the use of this book.

Contents

Introduction

The *American Heritage Dictionary* defines voodoo as "a religious cult of African origin characterized by a belief in sorcery and fetishes and rituals in which participants communicate by trance with ancestors, saints, or animistic deities."

This is an overly broad definition that begs further explanation. Voodoo came to America with the slaves who were brought from West Africa to the South to work the plantations. Brought into the country through the ports of Savannah and Charleston, many ended up in the Lowcountry on one of the three dozen biggest sea islands around South Carolina and Georgia, or in one of the surrounding communities. Many were Gullahs, who came from what are now known as Angola, Gambia, Liberia, Nigeria, and Senegal. The Gullahs brought their folklore, traditions, and beliefs with them.

Gullahs practice a unique blend of Christianity, herbalism (herbal medicine), and folk magic (which many consider to be the same as black magic). They believe, for instance, in both conjuration and Christianity. Black magic is often considered to be another word for voodoo, but not all voodoo is the same. What the Gullahs practice—called "vodoun" in western Africa, where the Gullah are originally from—is not the same as the hard-core voodoo or "vodou" performed in the Caribbean (particularly Haiti) and New Orleans, or the "Santería" practiced in Cuba. I grew up in the Lowcountry, where most everyone calls what the Gullah practice "Lowcountry voodoo," though it is officially known as "hoodoo."

Most of us are familiar with John Berendt's best-selling book *Midnight in the Garden of Good and Evil.* One of his most intriguing

About the Gullah

Where does the word "Gullah" come from? That is widely disputed. Some believe "Gullah" was shortened from "Angola," a region on the West African Coast. Some believe that the term derives from a Liberian group, the "Golas," who also come from the West African Coast. Still others believe Gullah was the language spoken by slaves and that the term later came to encompass their culture and way of life, as well.

characters is a voodoo priestess known as Minerva. In truth, she was based on real-life hoodoo practitioner (also called a conjurer or root doctor) Valerie Fennel Aiken Boles. As this example illustrates, there is widespread confusion on the subject of voodoo.

The most likely reason for this is that all of these practices (vodou, vodoun, hoodoo, and voodoo) are similar in many ways. Each uses conjuring, spells and charms, rituals, and herbs or roots to achieve results. And in each, a practitioner asks a deity, spirit, or ancestor for a specific result and expects results at the end of a performed ritual. (This is discussed further in the Special Spells chapter.) Despite what some say, if there is conjuring involved, black magic is being used, at least in my opinion. Some prefer to call this African-American "folk magic."

The biggest difference between Lowcountry voodoo and voodoo practiced elsewhere is that, unlike the forms practiced in other parts of the world, Lowcountry voodoo is not a religion. Even in regard to those forms of voodoo considered religions, however, there are experts who argue that voodoo is more of a spiritual system that uses rituals to get results than it is a religion. It's interesting to note that in Haiti the majority of the population is Catholic, yet just about everyone practices voodoo, despite the fact the Church denounces it. According to some experts, neither traditional voodoo nor Lowcountry voodoo are religions but just a series of steps for getting in touch with the spirit world using conjuring. Some suggest that Lowcountry voodoo is nothing more than a corruption of voodoo. Others say they are nothing alike. I'll leave it to the experts to debate this matter.

The goal of any kind of voodoo is for supernatural forces to improve the lives of those who practice it by helping them gain power in whatever area of their life they need help. Rituals may be performed to improve health; bring love, luck, or money; or to help a person get revenge. Herbs, minerals, incense, anointing oils, sachet powders, bath crystals, candles, roots, a person's possessions, and/or animal parts (such as a feather or claw) may be used to create a charm. Scripture from the Bible, such as psalms, may be recited during a hoodoo ritual.

While it is difficult for most of us to reconcile Christianity with sorcery, it is important to recognize that Gullahs are Christians who have blended their African heritage with their lives here in America.

The Gullahs believe that illness originates from spiritual evil, so medicine alone cannot cure those afflicted. This is why black or folk magic is used. Those who perform these rituals are called witch doctors, conjurers, or sorcerers. Since those terms carry negative connotations nowadays in law enforcement, the medical community, and mainstream religious sects, conjurers have begun calling themselves "root doctors." There is no law prohibiting the casting or removing of spells; however, dispensing medicines such as potions, oils, and gris-gris bags is illegal.

Gullahs believe that it is not enough to say that you believe in the Lord—you must show your sincerity by going through a process known as "seeking" (in which you ask for or seek the salvation of your soul) before the church will accept you. A spiritual leader or teacher is assigned to a seeker for this process. The spiritual leader serves as a mentor, making sure that the seeker spends sufficient time praying, fasting, and meditating in isolation.

When the spiritual teacher is certain that the seeker is ready and has "come tru," the leader will let the church elders know. The seeker is then baptized and the "presider" comes to the church to lead the service. The presider is the equivalent of a Catholic bishop. Singing is a big part of this service, as well as their religion. Old spirituals, hymns, and modern gospel tunes are sung in Gullah churches (also called praise houses). The "Ring Shout" is a popular ritual that involves dancing and shouting praises to God.

The Gullahs believe that the soul leaves the body when a person dies and returns to God. The spirit, however, remains on earth to intercede when necessary with the lives of the loved ones it has left behind. A spirit can be good or bad, protecting its family or tormenting those it chooses. The spirit that torments is the dreaded boo hag or haint. Elaborate funeral services are given to pay respect to the dead. Small children are passed over the coffin in the belief that the ritual protects them from the dead. Prized possessions are placed on the gravesite to show respect and appease the deceased. This is done to keep the dead from returning. Broken dishes are usually placed on the grave to signify the "chain" of death has been broken.

Today, there are about 150,000 Gullahs or Geechees in the Georgia–South Carolina area (although some sources inaccurately list the population as high as 500,000). They are called Gullahs in South Carolina and Geechees in Georgia.

As slaves, they rarely received medical care, so they depended on home remedies using medicinal plants and herbs. Even after slavery was abolished, they continued to treat themselves due to the scarcity of doctors and their isolation on these islands. These herbal remedies would be considered alternative medicine today. They were used for everything from injuries to illness. One such medicine was "Life Everlasting" (also called "Life Alasses"), an herbal cold medicine. The chest rub is made from whiskey, lemon, and turpentine. This effective remedy was extremely popular during a major flu outbreak. It could also be used to keep a person in good health, like taking a multi-vitamin. In these cases, the leaves, stem, and flowers of the plant are boiled and drunk like tea. Sea myrtle could be added. For those seeking relief from asthma, the dried plant could be smoked. Chewing the crumbled leaves could get rid of a toothache,

The Lowcountry

What exactly is the "Lowcountry"? This term describes the low-lying coastal areas (including the Sea Islands) of South Carolina, Georgia, and a little piece of extreme-northeast Florida. It is widely believed to begin at Charleston and extend to just below Savannah. However, if the definition is loosely applied, the Lowcountry can encompass all areas in South Carolina that are below the state's fall line, where the Upcountry meets the coastal plain. This would include Clarendon, Georgetown, Horry, Lee, Orangeburg, Sumter, and Williamsburg counties.

and bathing in it could help with foot pain and dry skin. Another example is sassafras tea, which is boiled from the plant's roots and used as a tonic and cold remedy. Many of these products were sold at the Charleston City Market up until the mid-1900s.

Gullahs still believe in herbal or alternative medicines for many illnesses. When something cannot be cured by these methods, a visit to a root doctor may be necessary. Root doctors (or witch doctors or conjurers) make "roots" using herbs and all kinds of strange items to cast spells and conjure good or evil.

While this book is first and foremost about Lowcountry voodoo, an understanding of the Gullahs is essential, as there would be no Lowcountry voodoo without them. Furthermore, I want to provide a sufficient explanation of their beliefs so as not to do them an injustice. I have set about this task with a great deal of respect and reverence for these people and their beliefs. Having lived in the South Carolina Lowcountry for much of my life, I have a healthy fascination for sea island history and folklore, which is why I have written several books on these subjects. I have always wanted to write a book devoted exclusively to Lowcountry voodoo. However, this book is not meant to be an exhaustive study of this complex subject, but rather a fun foray into an intriguing topic.

I hope you will enjoy *Lowcountry Voodoo: Beginner's Guide to Tales, Spells and Boo Hags.* You'll learn all about the inscrutable Dr. Buzzard, the creepy Boo Hag Bride, the apothecary who got more than he bargained for with his magic show, how to use voodoo dolls to get what you want, what you need to make a love charm, and much more. But beware! Black magic is not something you should play around with unless you're prepared to accept the consequences!

Gullah Beliefs

Health, Money, Dreams, Love, Death & Curses, and Luck

The Gullah people have always believed strongly in signs and rituals, and they pass these beliefs and traditions on to their kin and to other superstitious folks, as well. An example of such beliefs being put to use is that doors and shutters have been painted bright blue by all those who believe it will ward off evil spirits. In earlier times, this particular shade was known as "Indigo Blue" because the paint was created using skimmings from indigo pots.

About Indigo

The leaves of plants belonging to the *Indigofera* genus (legume plants that look a lot like alfalfa) are commonly the source of natural indigo dye, which must be made using an exact process that lasts a month. After being harvested, the indigo plants are soaked in water and allowed to ferment in vats. This separates the dyestuff from the plant. The dyestuff or solution is beaten (to oxidize it) and the excess water is then poured off. The sludge is dried and packed into cakes or patties. The skimmings are used to make Indigo Blue paint.

Here are some additional examples of Gullah beliefs:

Health

- Rheumatism can be cured by putting a potato in your pocket.

- For general ailments, you should tie a dime with a hole in it around your ankle.

- To get rid of a headache, you should tie a string around your head.

- Tie a piece of cotton around your left ankle to prevent swimmer's cramps.

Money

- If your right hand itches, it means you will receive a letter; if your left hand itches, it means you will receive money.

- If you see a red bird on your doorstep, count to nine and money will follow.

- Bubbles in your coffee mean that money is on the way.

- Dreams of running water mean good luck and money.

Dreams

- Wishes made to a new moon will come true, as will dreams had beneath a new quilt.

- If you dream about snakes, you will face some kind of temptation.

- If you dream that a deceased loved one or acquaintance asks you to give him or her something, you are not supposed to do it. Answering the request would be the same as giving yourself over to death.

Love

- Burn your ex-lover's shoes and you'll soon have more admirers.

- Pin a piece of your lover's shirt to your skirt to keep him or her true.

- Dreams of gray horses mean someone you know will soon get married.

Death & Curses

The Gullah are especially superstitious about death. Mirrors are turned to the wall so that the corpse won't be reflected. Those in the funeral party must wait outside the cemetery gate to ask their ancestors permission to enter. Toward the end of a funeral, small children are passed over the casket to prevent evil spirits from coming back to haunt them. Some folks believe that only babies need to be passed over the coffin, but others believe all small children should be protected. Some say it should be done graveside, while others are adamant the child should be passed over the coffin before it is lowered into the ground.

The Gullahs believe in placing items that belonged to the deceased on his or her grave. If you visit a Gullah cemetery, you'll find cups, utensils, jugs, and medicine bottles there. The Gullah place the last cup and saucer used by the deceased on the grave, alongside medicine bottles. If there is any medication left in a bottle, it is turned upside down so the contents will be absorbed into the grave. At a baby's grave, you'll find bottles and a pacifier resting there. The idea is to keep the spirit of the deceased content. Some believe that means leaving the most valuable or treasured item from home, such as an antique clock or good china.

The clock should be stopped at the time of death. A big meal called "saraka" is prepared after the funeral, and a plate set out for the deceased. The house should not be swept until the deceased is removed. If a husband dies first, his wife has to wear all black clothing for six months. If a wife dies first, her husband does not need to wear mourning clothes.

- Never shake hands. It will put a curse on both persons. (Some sources say you can shake hands so long as you never use the left hands, in which case, both parties would have to extend their right hands.)

- If a rooster crows at night, someone you know will die.

- Never let your photo be taken because the camera will steal your soul.

- If you hear someone call out to you, don't answer until you see someone there. You don't want to be conversing with a ghost!

- A malfunctioning clock striking thirteen is a sure sign of imminent death.

- A hooting owl is a bad omen (usually signifying death). You can stop the owl by crossing your fingers, taking off a shoe and turning it over, pointing your finger in the direction of the owl (or the sound if you don't see the owl), putting a poker in the fire, and squeezing your right wrist with your left hand. Or, if you happen to be outside and barefoot, you can simply point your finger at the owl or the noise. This should stop the hooting and cancel the bad omen.

- A howling dog outside means somebody you know is dying.

- It is bad luck to sweep after sundown. The reasoning behind this is that good spirits are believed to visit at night and you may accidentally sweep them out.

Luck

- Never try on someone else's hat or let someone wear your hat; it is bad luck.

- Never let someone comb your hair, because this, too, is bad luck.

- Don't throw away hair caught in your comb or brush, or you'll go crazy. After you finish brushing or combing your hair, the brush or comb should be buried in a hole near the house, burned, or flushed down the toilet.

- Stomping your left foot is bad luck; stomping your right is good luck.

- If you break a mirror, it will bring seven years of bad luck.

- If you find a coin facing "heads up," pick it up and throw it over your right shoulder for good luck.

- If you find a coin "tails up," leave it alone or you'll have bad luck.

- A horseshoe over your front door is good luck and keeps evil spirits away. It should always be hung to look like the letter "U" so that the luck doesn't run out.

- If you stub a toe on your left foot, stop and then turn to the right in a full circle for good luck. Do the opposite if you stub a toe on the right foot.

- Two or more people should not look in the mirror at the same time. If this happens, the youngest person looking will be the first to die.

- If a black cat walking down a road or path crosses in front of you heading toward your left, you will have bad luck that day.

- Walking backward is bad luck.

- If you wake up on the first day of the month and say "rabbit" before you get out of bed, it will be a good month.

- Never carry out fireplace ashes on Fridays or between Christmas and New Year's Day because it is bad luck.

- Never start a new task on Friday or you won't ever finish it.

- Never cut out a sewing pattern on Friday because it is bad luck.

- Never keep a crowing hen because it is bad luck.

- Never carry a hoe or spade into the house because it is bad luck.

- Lending matches is bad luck.

- Dreaming of chickens is bad luck.

- Never mend clothes while they're being worn because it is bad luck.

- Sleeping with your hands clasped behind your head is bad luck.

- If you're on your way somewhere and have to return home to get something you forgot, you must make an "X" in the road before turning around or something bad will happen during your journey.

- The first time you sleep in a strange house, make a wish and it will come true.

New Year's Day Traditions

A popular New Year's Day tradition, at least in the South, calls for serving a meal of collard greens, roast pork, and Hoppin' John. According to folklore, the pork ensures good health. Eating collard greens and Hoppin' John is said to bring wealth. The greens symbolize paper money while the peas in Hoppin' John represent coins. The idea is that such a menu will lead to a very blessed year. We get this tradition from the Gullahs, who actually put a few more traditions into practice that day so as to leave nothing to chance. Follow the steps below to learn a bit more about how the Gullahs celebrate New Year's.

After the supper dishes are removed, put a dollar bill and a silver dollar on the kitchen table. Place a green candle on top of the bill and silver dollar. Around the candle, place the leftover pork, greens, and Hoppin' John. Then, with salt and any other seasonings used to prepare the meal, draw a circle around the whole area. Light the candle and let it burn until it flickers out on its own. It is best to use a candle encased in glass because it is dangerous to leave a burning candle unattended. (That is true throughout this book whenever there is discussion of leaving a candle burning unattended.) While it is lit, recite prayers of prosperity. Leave all these items on the table overnight. In the morning, throw the salt seasoning mix and candle remains out the front door to chase away bad luck.

Some also put a silver dollar or dime into the pot of collard greens, in which case whoever ends up with that coin will have good luck all year.

Gullah Recipes

The following are the recipes needed to assemble a traditional New Year's Day meal. Okra soup, red rice, sweet potato pie, Lowcountry seafood boil, sweet bread, island shrimp creole, and gumbo are also popular Gullah dishes.

Southern Collard Greens

a bundle (or a "mess," as Southerners say) of collards
2 tbsp. olive oil or fatback (sliced thin & fried crisp to render the fat for the greens)
salt
garlic salt
pepper

Be sure to use tender, young leaves that are bright green in color. Remove imperfect leaves and root ends. Cut tender stems into ½-inch pieces and cook with the greens, as they will sweeten the leaves. If buying from a farmer's market or if they are picked fresh from the fields, wash the greens several times in water, lifting them out of the water each time so that any sand sinks to bottom. Drain. Wash and remove the tough, central ribs of the collard leaves, but only if they are old and tough. Chop leaves. Bring a large pot of water (with just enough water to cover the greens) to a boil and drop collards in. Boil for 45 minutes and then drain by lifting collards out of pot and into a frying pan (do not drain excess water from collards, as it is needed in frying pan). Add olive oil (or grease from several pieces of fatback that have been fried crisp) and simmer on medium heat for twenty minutes or so, stirring often and tasting for desired consistency. Sprinkle in salt, garlic salt, and pepper to suit your tastes. Serve immediately, if desired, or cool and then put them in the refrigerator to be heated in the microwave the next day. Many collard lovers argue that they are better the next day.

Optional: At the table, some folks like to add hot sauce or pass around a vinegar cruet containing vinegar that has been allowed to absorb the heat and the flavor of small, whole hot red or green peppers which have been left in the liquid. Another option would be to add a little lemon juice, some crispy fried bacon bits, or grated Parmesan cheese just as the greens are ready to serve.

However you serve them, don't forget to slip in a dime or silver dollar for good luck for the lucky recipient!

West African Influences

The Gullah brought their traditions, recipes, and beliefs with them from West Africa. Here are a few examples of how West African culture has had an impact on Gullah culture:

- Gullah red rice is similar to African Jollof rice.

- Gullah gumbo is similar to African okra soup.

- A Gullah root doctor is similar to an African medicine man or witch doctor.

- Gullah herbal medicines are similar to African remedies.

- The Gullah "plateye" is similar to the African "cymbee."

Hoppin' John

1 cup small dried beans (usually black-eyed peas)

5 ½ cups water

1 dried hot pepper (optional)

1 smoked ham hock

1 onion, chopped (about 1 cup)

1 cup long-grain white rice

Wash the beans/peas thoroughly, put them in a saucepan, and add water. Some recommend getting rid of any peas that float because they are inferior. Gently boil the (uncovered) peas with the hot pepper, ham hock, and onion until tender. Be careful not to let them get mushy. If they were soaked several hours or overnight, the beans will be ready in about one hour. (And if they were soaked, be sure to pour out that water and add fresh water to cook them in.) Check after 40 or 45 minutes, as they might be ready sooner. Add the rice, cover the pot, and let the beans simmer on low heat for 20 minutes. Remove from heat but do not uncover; let stand and steam for 10 minutes. Remove the lid, stir slightly with a fork, and serve immediately.

Note: The smoked ham hock is traditional and gives the dish added flavor, but it can be left out if you're a vegetarian or have health concerns.

Pork and Hoppin' John Jambalaya

This dish has has everything you need for that traditional meal except the collards. Serves six.

8 oz. smoked sausage, sliced ½-inch thick

1 lb. lean pork chunks, cut into 1-inch cubes

1 tsp. Cajun seasoning

¼ cup oil

1 cup diced onion

¼ cup diced bell pepper

¼ cup diced celery

1 cup water

1 cup chicken broth

¼ cup butter or margarine

¼ tsp. salt

¼ tsp. black pepper

¼ tsp. ground cayenne pepper

1 cup uncooked long grain rice

1 (15 oz.) can black-eyed peas, drained

In a Dutch oven, brown sausage and pork in hot oil. Season with Cajun seasoning. Add onion, bell pepper, and celery. Cover and cook over medium heat 20 to 30 minutes (or until pork is nearly done). Skim off excess fat. Add water, broth, butter, salt, and peppers. Bring mixture to a boil. Add rice and black-eyed peas, stirring to blend. Cover and cook 25 to 30 minutes (or until rice is cooked).

Southern Cornbread

Eating them is not necessarily considered good luck, but cornbread and biscuits are Southern staples. Cornbread goes great with the special New Year's meal.

2 cups yellow cornmeal

1 ½ cups flour

2 tsp. salt

2 tsp. baking powder

1 tsp. baking soda

3 eggs, beaten

2 cups milk

¼ cup melted butter

1 tbsp. vegetable oil for skillet

melted butter for brushing top

Preheat oven to 425°. Put oil in a 10-inch iron skillet and place in the oven to preheat. In a large bowl, mix cornmeal, flour, salt, baking powder, and baking soda. In another bowl, whisk the eggs, milk, and butter. Add this to the bowl of dry ingredients and stir until mixture is the consistency of pancake batter. Don't overmix; batter is supposed to be a little lumpy. As soon as the oven temperature reaches 425° (to ensure a crisp, delicious crust), remove the skillet from the oven and pour the batter into it before returning the skillet to the oven. Bake for about twenty minutes or until brown. Insert a toothpick into the center to test it. If it comes out clean, the cornbread is ready. Brush with melted butter and you won't even have to butter the cornbread at the table.

Southern Buttermilk Biscuits
   2 cups all-purpose flour
   2 ½ teaspoons baking powder
   ¼ teaspoon baking soda
   1 teaspoon salt
   ¼ cup lard or vegetable shortening
   2 tablespoons butter
   ¾ cup buttermilk

Make sure the oven rack is in the center position and preheat oven to 450°. With this position in the oven, you'll need to watch the bottoms of biscuits carefully, as they may brown more quickly than the tops in some ovens.

In a large bowl, mix flour, baking powder, baking soda, and salt. Cut in lard/shortening and butter until the pieces resemble peas. Pour buttermilk into middle of mixture and begin mixing until it clumps together as dough. Add 2 to 3 more teaspoons of buttermilk if necessary. Transfer dough to a lightly floured board, turn dough over on the flour, and lightly sprinkle with additional flour if sticking. Then knead several times, being careful not to handle dough much, as it will make biscuits tough. Roll out a circle 6 to 8 inches in diameter and ½-inch thick. Cut using biscuit cutter and place on greased bread pan (pan with ½" sides) or baking sheet. Bake for ten minutes or until the tops are browned.

Rice and Malaria

Most Lowcountry recipes call for rice because it is a staple in the Lowcountry. This was especially true during the era of rice plantations. South Carolina, then part of what was simply "Carolina," was founded by King Charles II in 1663. The land was given to eight Lords Proprietor for their service to the king. Because of the climate and terrain of the Lowcountry, it was perfect for growing Sea Island cotton, indigo, and rice. Slaves were brought to the area from West Africa because of their expertise in cultivating rice.

The slave ships also brought mosquitoes, however. The swampy Lowcountry and soggy rice fields were perfect breeding grounds for the malaria-carrying insects. Malaria became an epidemic. At that time, the plantation owners didn't know what caused the disease. They only knew that they needed to pack up and leave the plantations during summer months. This was later dubbed the "white flight." The slaves were remarkably immune to malaria, so they were left under the supervision of an overseer. This isolation contributed significantly to the survival of their way of life.

When the owners' families *were* home, dinner was served on most plantations at 3 P.M., and rice was almost always on the menu. It was even used in bread and desserts.

Lowcountry Rice Pudding

    ½ cup long-grain rice (must be long-grain)

    $1/_3$ cup light or dark brown sugar

    ½ tsp. pure vanilla extract

    ½ tsp. salt

    ¼ tsp. nutmeg

    ¼ tsp. cinnamon

    ¾ cup seedless raisins

    1 quart milk

    1 tsp. grated lemon peel (optional)

Preheat oven to 300°. Rinse rice. Then mix rice, milk, brown sugar, and salt. Pour mixture into a baking dish. Bake for about an hour, stirring as needed. Remove from oven and add nutmeg, cinnamon, vanilla, raisins, and lemon peel, stirring well. Put back in oven and bake 1–1 ½ hours. Makes six good servings.

Special Spells

There are two basic ways to conjure. Black magic can be combined with either charms or voodoo dolls. Black magic is the ritual performed to enable a charm or voodoo doll to work. Neither charms nor voodoo dolls will be effective without some kind of ritual having been performed beforehand. The ritual varies according to what kind of charm or doll you are making.

> ## What Is a Root?
>
> A root is the same as a charm or mojo or gris-gris. It can be worn, chewed, buried, or carried, depending on what the conjurer advises. Some, like the "Love Me" charm, have standard ingredients, while others may be custom-made depending on how they will be used.

Charms

Charms are called many different things, such as gris-gris bags, conjure bags, ouanga bags, mojo bags, or simply charms. They are filled with many things: herbs, roots, powders, stones, feathers, bones, cloth, and personal items (hair, used tissues, nail trimmings, photographs, etc.). Other items that can be used in making these charms include four-leaf clovers, a rabbit's foot, dice, parchment talismans, patron saint medals, coins, and a small crucifix.

- Four-leaf clovers or a rabbit's foot represent good luck.
- A small crucifix symbolizes faith.
- Coins represent wealth.
- Dice can symbolize wealth and good luck.
- Talismans and patron saint medals provide protection.

My research revealed that some conjurers believe that anointing oil must be used on the outer edge of the charm bag. So, if one is putting together a love charm, a love oil should be applied to the outside of the bag. If the charm is for protection, protection oil is used. And so forth.

The number of items used to make a charm is 1, 3, 5, 7, 9, or 13. There should never be an even number of objects, nor should there ever be more than thirteen items in a bag.

A ritual, which includes chanting, is performed as the items are placed in the bag. Chanting is done in a soft voice, never high-pitched or loud. The conjurer may perform the ritual on his or her own and then give you the gris-gris bag with instructions, or he or she may have you attend the ritual and participate.

A woman would then pin the charm inside her bra or under her shirt near the left armpit, while a man would wear the bag around his neck, pinned to the inside of his underwear, or simply inside his pocket so he could touch the bag frequently. This depends on the instructions given by the conjurer.

There are many types of charms, such as those meant to protect your home, ensure your health and prosperity, help you find love, keep you safe from evil, etc. I'm only going to include one example here (you will understand why when you see how intricate it is!).

The following information was compiled using several sources. See References in the back of this book for more information.

Getting Ready

Step One: Items Needed to Make a Charm

Note: As mentioned, I am only going to discuss how to make one particular charm. I chose to include only one charm because, as you will see, it is a lengthy and complicated process. I have randomly chosen the Love Charm, but there are many, including Health, Money, and Getting Rid of an Enemy.

For a Love Charm, or to get someone to fall in love with you

There is not much information available regarding exact ingredients and procedures for rituals like this. In any case, my research indicates that it is not so much what ingredients are used as the strength of a person's belief in the ritual's power that is important. If you believe, it will happen. If you are skeptical, it doesn't matter what you do—it won't happen. So, these items and steps are more symbolic (according to some) than essential. That said, there are voodoo practitioners who believe amateurs should never mess around with conjuring.

For the Love Charm, you will need:

>   1 red "bride and groom" candle (candle carved in the shape of a bride and groom) or round, red candle
>
>   Love Me anointing oil (such as jasmine, lavender, and virgin olive oil)
>
>   Love Me incense (such as frankincense and rose petals) and incense burner

Love Me bath crystals

Love Me sachet powder

Pair of lodestones

Packet of magnetic sand

Packet of mixed "Love Me" herbs (such as spikenard and damiana)

John the Conqueror root

Queen Elizabeth root

Red flannel bag

Cloth or string tie for the flannel bag with a heart charm attached (The heart can be metal, plastic, rubber, or whatever—it is merely being used as a symbol of your love)

Personal item of person you desire and a personal item of your own

Note: You can find a few shops in the Lowcountry, especially in Charleston and Savannah, that sell these items. There may even be places online to buy them. If you are interested in making a charm, you should buy the packaged Love Me incense and other necessary ingredients.

Step Two: Preparing for the Ritual

There are certain steps that must be done always, regardless of what kind of charm is being created. Every ritual must begin with a dark, quiet room. The only light should be from the candles on the altar. I

About Lodestones

Lodestones are naturally occurring magnets that are made of magnetized pieces of the mineral known as magnetite You can find these in stores that sell these kinds of items. Some argue that, for a charm ritual, an everyday magnet will work just as well, and that lodestones aren't even necessary. The general thinking is that they can't hurt, so why not use them? The more powerful you can make a charm, the better, so using lodestones is like erring on the side of caution. Bigger lodestones are used for money and luck charms, while smaller lodestones are used for love charms. If the instructions call for a pair, that means a male and female lodestone. To represent a male, you need a pointed lodestone, and for the female, a rounded lodestone is used. Some practitioners recommend dressing the stones with anointing oil and sprinkling them with magnetic sand.

have seen some pretty specific information regarding how to arrange the altar in books such as Ray T. Malbrough's *Charms, Spells, & Formulas*, but this is not as important (according to some) as the belief in the process.

To begin the ritual, you should first bathe in a bath with some Love Me bath crystals dissolved in it. Fill a jug with water from your bath and save it. Dry off with clean towel and put on clean clothes. As you dress, sprinkle Love Me sachet powder on your body and inside your shoes. Also, sprinkle the four corners of your room and between your box spring and mattress with the powder. After you have dressed, go outside and throw the water in the jug to the east. Turn around and walk home without looking back. As you sprinkle the powder in your bedroom and toss out the water, you may say a few well-chosen words. Be sure to mention your name and the name of the person whose love you desire. You need only perform this part of the ritual on the first day.

Also on the first day, you will need to divide the remaining ingredients so as to allow you to repeat the process described below each day.

Fill the incense burner with Love Me incense and light it. Use a marker to write your own name and the name of the one you desire on the side of the "bride and groom" candle, then dress the candle with Love Me anointing oil each day. This is done by rubbing a light coat of the oil along the sides of the candle. The anointed candle should burn throughout the daily process, including the bath on that first day. Place the lodestones some distance apart on the altar.

The rest of the ingredients (such as the sachet powder, Queen Elizabeth root, and remaining magnetic sand) will go inside the red flannel bag. You should say a few words or chant while inserting the items and before tying the bag closed with the cloth or string tie. Again, what you say is not as important as wholeheartedly believing in what you are doing. When casting out evil, a person may choose to recite the Bible's Psalm 23. When doing a Love Charm, a person may choose to recite a love poem or song lyrics, or to just speak from the heart about his or her feelings.

On each of the next six days, dress the candle and then light it and the incense, pray or chant over the charm bag, and then dress the lodestones with magnetic sand and move them closer together so that by the seventh day they are touching, snuffing out the candle and incense afterward. On the final day, put the lodestones in the bag, dress it with love oil, and then carry it around with you until the spell takes effect.

Step Three: When You're Done
After completing the ritual on the seventh day, you should save the remains of the ingredients: candle wax, incense ashes, and sachet powders. Put these items in a tiny bag or piece of cloth. Write your name and the name of your loved one on a piece of paper and add this to the bag. Tie it tightly and bury it in your backyard. Again, you may opt to say a few appropriate words as you do this final step of your love charm.

More About Charms
How many charms are there? More than you can imagine! There are charms for just about any situation. Need a job? Get the Steady Work Charm. Have a gambling problem? Try the Stop Gambling Charm! Below are some more examples. You will notice that several are similar, but none are the same. There are probably about a dozen love charms alone.

Attraction Charm: used to attract something a person wants, such as luck, love, or money

Breakup Charm: used when someone wants to get rid of his or her lover

Cast Off Evil Charm: used to ward off the evil eye

Hot Foot Charm: used to drive away any unwanted person, such as a bad neighbor or ex-lover

Fast Luck Charm: used to bring a person luck in a hurry for gambling, business, love, or money

John the Conqueror Charm: used to improve luck and to increase money, personal power, and virility

King Solomon Wisdom Charm: used to increase wisdom for making important decisions

Kiss Me Charm: used by those who want good sex but not necessarily love

Law Keep Away: used to keep the authorities away, such as the IRS or the ICE

Money Charm: used to bring wealth

Peaceful Home Charm: used to improve marital harmony

Psychic Vision Charm: used to develop a person's psychic abilities

Real Estate Charm: used by those trying unsuccessfully to sell their home

Reconciliation Charm: used by those wanting to reunite with a lover or spouse

Stay With Me Charm: used by those wanting guaranteed fidelity

Steady Work Charm: used to gain employment or by a person who wants to hold on to a job amid concern that he or she might soon get fired or laid off

Uncrossing Charm: used to end bad luck or to break a jinx

Voodoo Dolls

These dolls should be made with cloth or clay. Some say it doesn't matter, but others say a clay doll should be made from clay found in a crayfish hole. A cloth doll, on the other hand, is a human outline made from two pieces of material and stuffed with anything from cotton or straw to Spanish moss or herbs. If the doll is supposed to look like a red-haired man, it should have red wool for hair. The same holds true for the eyes—if the doll is meant to resemble someone with blue eyes, blue thread should be used for the pupils. The cloth should be an article of used or soiled clothing worn by the person the doll is supposed to resemble. The doll does not have to look exactly like the person the black magic will be used on, but at the very least the person making the doll should have a clear image of that person in his or her mind throughout the creation of the doll.

Simply making the doll is not enough. A ritual must be performed, one that includes a chant and that requires creating an altar using candles, incense (and incense burner), flowers, dirt from Mother Earth, Holy Water, and the doll. The doll should remain wrapped in clean, white linen until your ritual. Candles can be made with special herbs to add potency to the ritual. For example, to curse someone you would use a black candle and roll the candle in powdered knot grass (or mix the herbs into the wax if you make your own candles).

Step One: What You'll Need

If you want to make someone fall in love with you, you may use a voodoo doll only or use a voodoo doll in conjunction with a love charm. For the latter you'll need:

Love Charm (see page 30)
1 voodoo doll representing the person wanting to be loved
1 voodoo doll representing the person whose love is desired
2 red candles
2 yellow candles
1 orange candle
love incense and incense burner
1 bottle of love oil
dirt and flowers from Mother Earth
Holy Water

Mariah's Voodoo Doll

There's a great story in *Tales of Edisto* (Nell Graydon, 1955) about Gullah beliefs. The author had a laundress, Toria, who became ill. Different treatments were tried, but Toria remained very sick. Graydon tried to take Toria to the doctor, but the woman refused.

"T'ain't no use, Missus," she said sadly. "I gwine see death. Beulah, 'e done hab ole Riah f'row spell puntop me. Jist yestiddy top do'step uh fin' dried toad. T'ain't no use."

(Translation: Toria believed that a female conjurer named Mariah had put a death curse on her on behalf of a woman named Beulah). Toria believed that Beulah was in love with her husband.

Having heard of Mariah (Riah) and her reputation for conjuring charms, Graydon went to the woman's cabin to ask her to leave Toria alone. She also gave her a bribe of two bags of tobacco and several small pieces of silver.

Mariah grinned and snatched the items, promising, "Fuh sutt'n, Missus, Riah help Toria. Tell she attuh w'ile she be well. Riah suh so."

(Translation: She promised Graydon that Toria would be fine soon).

The message was delivered to Toria and, sure enough,

the woman was soon well. When Toria's husband, Bi'man, complained of chest pains, Toria begged Graydon to intercede again. The couple was convinced that Beulah was angry that Bi'man had resisted her advances and had gotten Mariah to cast another spell or hex, this time on Bi'man instead of Toria.

Once more, Graydon rode down the long sand road to Riah's cabin and took bribes—tobacco and a bag of groceries. After examining the items Graydon had brought, Riah nodded her approval and then pulled a man-shaped doll from an old chest. A string was wrapped tightly around the doll's chest, and as the woman unwound the cord that smelled strongly of kerosene, she instructed Graydon to take the doll to Toria. If she kept the doll safe, no spirits would ever harm her family. Almost immediately after Graydon delivered the doll to the couple and told them what the conjurer had promised, Bi'man's pains stopped.

*As discussed when making charms, you should find a place that sells love incense and love oil rather than try to make it yourself. There are shops in the Lowcountry (and probably online) that sell these items.

Step Two: The Candles

While setting up the altar, write the names of the dolls on the red candles and then coat them with love oil. Tie the candles to the dolls using red thread. Light the incense burner and allow it to burn during the ritual. When you light the first red candle, chant something appropriate about how great your love is for this person, making sure to say your name and that of the one whose love you desire.

Coat the two yellow candles with love oil and light them. Say the name of your beloved at least three times. Next, light the orange candle. While doing so, think about the life you want with this person. Picture the two of you happily together forever. Let the candles burn for one hour and then blow them out in the reverse order they were lit.

Repeat this ritual daily, moving the two dolls 1–2 inches closer to each other each time until the dolls touch. On the last day, bind the dolls together with red ribbon. Then, wrap them in white linen and put them in a safe place.

When to Perform Rituals

The day you perform the ritual is important. Each day is ruled by a different planet and thus has a unique astrological meaning. For example, Sunday is ruled by the sun, which is often represented by the color yellow. Yellow is associated with peace and harmony, so rituals performed on Sunday should be about friendship and the recovery of lost things or relationships.

Monday is ruled by the moon (white). White symbolizes love and fertility. Logically, then, a love charm ritual should be performed on a Monday (or Friday, as we'll see below).

Tuesday is ruled by Mars (red). Rituals done on that day should thus involve acting with courage, stopping enemies, and breaking curses.

Wednesday is ruled by Mercury (purple), meaning the most successful rituals on this day are those concerning health, spiritual well-being, and the attempt to influence others.

Thursday is ruled by Jupiter (blue). Rituals on this day should be about wealth, luck, and ambition.

Friday is ruled by Venus (green), which influences love, happiness, lust, and romance.

Finally, Saturday is ruled by Saturn (black). Only rituals regarding evil, negativity, and the protection of a person's home from these bad things should be performed.

Folk Spells

There's another kind of spell that is completely different from those previously discussed—a folk spell. It requires a brief ritual, an altar is not necessary, herbs are rarely used, and no chanting or words are necessary.

Examples of Folk Spells

To Obtain the One You Desire

Take a mirror your loved one has looked into, but that you have never used. Do not to look into it as you break it into several pieces. Be careful not to cut yourself as you collect these pieces, put them into a bag, and bury the bag in your yard (under your bedroom window if possible). Sprinkle the place were you buried the bag with a traditional love herb, such as lavender, mistletoe, spikenard, or rose hips. You can do this anytime, but since the best days of the week for love rituals are Mondays and Fridays, I recommend those days. Do this until the one you desire responds the way you want.

To Defeat an Enemy

Write your enemy's name on a pink or brown candle, writing either on the candle itself with a marker or on a label to be attached to the candle. One hour before you go to bed, light the candle and declare yourself rid of your enemy. Be sure to include the name of your enemy. You can say something as simple as "John Smith will no longer be a problem for me." Blow out the candle before you fall asleep. Do this each night until the candle is nearly gone. Bury what's left of the candle in your backyard on a Saturday, again reciting that your enemy will no longer plague you.

To Get Rid of Someone

On a piece of paper, write down the name of the person you want to be rid of an odd number of times, such as 3,5, or 9. Put the paper in a jar. Fill the jar with vinegar, screw the lid on, and throw it into a body of water, such as an inlet, river, or lake. Note that this charm is different from one you would use on an enemy. The target of this charm can be a pesky neighbor or co-worker, or a lover you no longer desire. Tuesday is a good day to perform this task.

Remarkable Tales

The Lowcountry is a sultry, seductive place known for plough mud and palmettos, graceful snowy egrets and huge herons, old fishing trawlers and extraordinarily expensive yachts, remote sea islands filled with tiny beach cottages and four-story mansions, low-lying marsh and miles of wetlands, fantastic sunsets and mosquitoes as big as your thumbnail, fascinating legends and peculiar folklore...and voodoo. No book on Lowcountry voodoo, in my opinion, would be complete without stories that emerge from this magic place, stories about creepy boo hags, witch doctors, haints, and evil plateyes. These are some of my favorite tales, which I learned while growing up in the Lowcountry and while writing this book.

The Boo Hag Bride

There once was a young man who wanted desperately to get married and have a family. He wasn't much to look at, but he was nice and worked hard. Despite his best efforts, though, he could not find a woman willing to be his bride.

He worked in his daddy's store six days a week, and during the many hours they worked together, the boy told his father about his woes.

"Pa, I jis don't get it. I done tried every single girl in da county. Not one of dem be interested. I f'aid I ain' nebbuh gonna git wed. I don my best sweetmouth but dat don't seem make no matter. I gonna go to me grabe alone."

The man's heart nearly broke at hearing how miserable his son was. He was a good boy and any woman would be lucky to have him. She just might need a little help realizing it.

"Isn't der a big dance tomorrow?" he asked.

"Yes, sir, dat be right, but I ain't going. Ain't no use," the boy answered.

"You change your mind, son. Don't give up. You go to dat dance."

"Yes, sir, if you say so."

He told his son he might be a little late for work the next day because he had something he had to do. He took his little boat up to the other side of the island, and as the sun was rising, he pulled up to his destination. A woman, leaning heavily on a cane, hobbled out of a shack to greet him.

"Lord, da sky must be falling in! What else would bring the likes of Mondie Robinson to my door?"

"Come now, Belah, it hasn't been that long," he said pleasantly.

"Gone on four years, for sure, since my beloved done been laid to rest."

"I can't b'leew how time flies. When my daddy used to say that, I thought it was a foolish thing to say. And now I find me saying it more and more!"

"Amen," she agreed. "Don't know where time done gone. My Toriah be eighteen tomorrow. You b'leew dat?"

"Hard to b'leew," he said. But he had done the math and already knew that. She had been a lovely fourteen-year-old girl when he saw her at her father's funeral four years ago. He had forgotten about her until he had racked his brains thinking of possible brides for his son. He was hoping she was not already promised, but didn't think she would be. Belah had not sent her off island to school, and they mostly kept to themselves. That didn't leave much chance that she'd been courted.

"How 'bout letting Toriah celebrate her birthday by going to a dance with my son?" he asked hopefully. He tried to sound casual, but Belah had always been good at reading minds.

"Hum! Do say, dat be why you're here? Your boy need a girl?" She crossed her arms in front of her chest and stared at him.

"Well, he be twenty now and getting to a dainjus age for a man to be alone. Don't want him getting into trouble without a good woman to watch after him."

She cocked her head and studied him for a long moment. "What's it be to me?"

"James is a good boy. I can say dat whole heart," the father said. "He's a good worker, too. Works long hours every day 'cept Sundays. Store closed for church. He gone git da store one day. He be able to give a woman all she needs. Dat no small thing. He don't drink, swear, or play cards. He be good husband."

"If he be so good, why he not already taken?" she asked.

"He ain't met the right woman yet. I b'leew God saving him for Toriah. And how could she do better? She ain't been schooled so she can't leave the island. There ain't many choices for her. She could have a good life. It'd be a weight off you, not to have to worry about her no more."

Belah stared up at the sky for a few seconds and then spoke. "Let me pray on it and I'll let you know by day's end."

The father could barely concentrate that day. He fretted all day about what the woman would say. After work, he took his little boat once again up the waterway to the other side of the island. When he pulled onto shore, he saw two women sitting on the porch of the shabby cabin.

"Child, I'd like you to meet an old friend of your daddy's. Dis here's Mr. Mondie Robinson. Do you 'member him from your

48

daddy's funeral?" Belah pushed the younger woman forward.

The daugher nodded her head. "Yes 'em, I sure do. Nice see you again, Mr. Robinson."

She was a beautiful girl. Well-defined cheekbones, soft brown eyes framed with lush lashes, flawless chocolate-colored skin, and a petite frame.

"Mr. Robinson gone 'vited you to a dance tonight. Go in and change to your best dress and comb your hair. He gone take you to the dance to meet his boy."

The girl seemed reluctant. She looked from him to her mother.

"Go on, child," she said. "It be all right. You have a good time. You'll see. I don laid your dress out. Be gone with you. Don't want to keep the boy waiting too long. A little wait is good for a man. Too long a wait makes a man lose interest!" She laughed, and the girl disappeared into the house.

Mondie laughed too. They sat and talked for a few minutes, until the door opened. Toriah, looking shy, slowly emerged. She had put on a pretty dress and Sunday shoes.

Her mother pulled a little pot from her pocket and twisted off the lid. She painted some of the red stuff onto her daughter's lips.

"Jis right. You mind yourself. I see you in a couple of hours," she told her daughter.

When they arrived at the little schoolhouse, Mondie led the girl inside. He found his son standing alone in the corner looking unhappy. He introduced them to each other and said he would be back in two hours to take them home.

James Robinson fell in love that night. He had chased many girls, but this was the first one he had truly loved. He finally knew what love was. They had a wonderful evening. They danced and drank sweet tea and talked about everything. In what seemed like no time at all, his father was back and the evening was over. He courted Toriah for two months before asking if she would marry him. Even though he knew right away she was the one he wanted to spend the rest of his life with, it took him two months to get his courage up to ask. What if she said no? He couldn't take it if she rejected him. But she didn't. She said yes and kissed him for the first time. He had brushed her cheek with a brief kiss a few times, but this was the first time that his lips had touched hers.

He did not want a long engagement, so they were married within three months of their first meeting. The young man had rented a cabin about a mile or so from the store. It had an extra bedroom so that her mother could come visit whenever she liked. Toriah had told him that one day when her mother was old and unable to care for herself, she may have to live with them. They settled into a comfortable routine. He went to work and she had dinner waiting for him every night. He liked seeing smoke coming out of the chimney and smelling the likes of spicy gumbo with big buttermilk biscuits and sweet cornbread with Frogmore stew as he approached their home. He finally had what he'd always dreamed of.

There was just one problem. He woke up sometimes during the night and discovered his wife was not there. When he asked her about it, she said that she often had trouble sleeping so she went into the kitchen or living room and knitted or sewed until she got tired. She didn't want to disturb his sleep since he worked so hard, she told him. That made sense until one night he found her missing from their bed and went looking for her. He was going to coax her back to bed, but couldn't find her anywhere. Alarmed, he began to dress to go look for her when she came into the bedroom.

She was startled to see her husband awake. When he asked where she had been, she refused to answer. He didn't know what to do. There was no good reason his wife would not tell him. Maybe she had gone off to meet another man? He longed to talk to his father but didn't dare. He didn't want his father to know he may already be having marital problems. He couldn't think who to talk to. He couldn't see himself unburdening himself to one of his friends. He wouldn't even know how to bring it up. He thought about talking to her mother but knew that was not a good idea. She had thought that they jumped into the marriage too soon. She had suggested that they be engaged for a year before getting married. He tried to forget about it but just couldn't. Something was going on, he felt sure, and he needed to do something.

He finally decided to go see the local conjurer. The woman was wise in these matters. If anyone could help, she could. He brought her two big bags of groceries. After she inspected them, she smiled and told him to sit down. He did so and then told her everything. She asked a few questions and then advised him.

"Don't go to sleep tonight. Make b'leew you be but stay awake. Go see what she do when she leaves you, but don't let her know it," she said.

That night, they went to bed as usual. Even though James was tired from lack of sleep and worrying, he made himself stay awake. After a half-hour or so, he felt her lift the covers off herself and slide out of bed. She softly padded across the room and left, quietly pulling the door shut behind her.

He waited a minute before following her. He opened the door slightly and gasped at what he saw. His wife was seated at her spinning wheel, spinning her skin off! It was an ugly sight, one that would haunt him forever. The bloodred mass with bulging blue veins floated away from the spinning wheel and out the living room window! He stumbled back to bed, barely able to make his feet shuffle over to it. He collapsed into the comfort of the big bed and pulled the quilt up to his chin. He was shivering uncontrollably, tingling with fear and trepidation. He must have worn himself out because he fell asleep. When he awoke, his wife was next to him. She was abnormally hot and sweaty but sleeping like the dead.

He slipped out of bed and quickly dressed. He fairly flew up the road to the conjurer's house. The words tumbled out of his mouth. He knew he wasn't making sense, but the old woman understood what he was saying.

"It be bad," she said shaking her head. "It be the worse kind of bad. You married a boo hag!"

"No, dat can't be. My Toriah is a sweet, kind woman. She ain't no witch! You dunno what you talking 'bout!" he screamed.

"You got to listen to me boy or she gone finish you off one of these days. The first night she can't find something else, she gone have to ride you and then eat your flesh and bones! You got to stop her. I can prove she's a boo hag easy as dat."

"How?" he asked.

"Tonight after she sheds her skin and disappears into the night, you paint all the outside doors and windows with dis here paint. When she tries to return before the morning light, she won't be able to on account of the protection paint around all the doors and windows she might use to get inside. But leave one window unpainted. After you see her try to get in but not able to 'cause she evil, you can do what needs to be done. When she finds the one unpainted window and flies inside, she'll go right to her skin to put it back on. But her skin will be full of salt you've put there and it will burn her. That will get rid of the boo hag! And dat be the only way, so heed my words," she said.

He took the can of paint with him. He hid it behind a chair on the porch. James and Toriah had dinner and went to bed soon after. Once again, he pretended to sleep but stayed awake. About a half-hour later, his wife left the bedroom. He couldn't help himself—he opened the door a crack and peeked out into the dark living room. A candle illuminated his wife. She was at her spinning wheel and her skin was falling off from head to toe as she pedaled. And then she was gone.

Like a rabbit, he ran across the floor and onto the porch. He jerked open the paint and grabbed the brush he had placed next to the can. He hurriedly threw bright blue paint on the trim around the front and back doors. Next, he painted all the windows except for a tiny one on the other side of the fireplace and threw the paint can and brush into the closet. He searched until he found the salt canister, and then he carried it over to the spinning wheel; he could barely look at the pile of skin scattered on the floor beside it. He gagged as he poured the entire contents of the can onto the skin. He threw the empty can into the closet alongside the paint and then sat down in a chair in the corner to wait.

As the darkness was giving way to dawn's early light, he heard his wife reach the porch. She tried the door, but it wouldn't open.

He could hear her whizzing all around the house trying to find a way inside. It was a horrible sound. She was running out of time and she knew it—the sun would be up any minute. She had to get into the house and into her skin before that happened. But the protection paint was working. Evil could not cross its threshold. Finally, she found the one window she could access. She slid it open and slithered inside. The grotesque creature grabbed her skin and put it on. As soon as she did, she let out a horrific howl. He watched as she disintegrated in front of him. He turned his head and averted his eyes until he was sure there was nothing left.

He never told anyone what really happened. He told people she left him, that she had taken off the previous day while he was at work and never come back. Only the conjurer knew the real story. When he took a chicken, a dozen fresh-laid eggs, and a bag of groceries to thank her for helping him, she put a tiny sack in his hand.

"Dis here be a love charm. Pin it to the inside of your shirt, over your heart. The next unmarried girl you meet with a pure heart will be yours," she instructed. "I done a ritual already."

He took the charm and did as she told him, but did not think anything would come of it. He had lost faith in love. Three days later, a pretty young woman came into the store.

"Hi, James. I heard 'bout Toriah. Just wanted to say how sorry I was."

"Thanks, Mariah," he said.

"I was wondering if you'd like to come over for Sunday supper?

My brother caught a whole mess of catfish and mama's gonna fry dem up crisp as a fritter. Be serving sweet potato pone too."

"Dat sounds too good to pass up. Thanks 'gain."

"I'll save you a seat next to me at church and then we can walk home together," she said shyly.

He smiled and removed the charm from his chest when she left. He didn't think he needed it anymore.

Boo Hags 101

Gullahs believe that people have both a soul and a spirit. Upon death, the soul leaves the body and ascends to Heaven—if it was a good soul. A good *spirit*, on the other hand, stays on earth and watches over the family, interceding when needed. A "boo hag" is a bad spirit who uses witchcraft to get a person to do what she wishes.

The scariest time to encounter a hag is at night. When darkness falls, she can shed her skin and become invisible, allowing her to go wherever she wants. Once inside a house, she will sit (or "ride") on her sleeping victim's chest. When the person wakes up, he or she is unable to remove the hag or summon help and can thus be choked or suffocated by the hag. You may not be able to see her, but you'll know when a boo hag is close by; the air becomes hot and moist and smells of rotting meat.

There are some things you can do to confuse and elude the dreadful boo hag, like place a broom by the door. Day or night, hags will not pass a broom by. They are curious creatures and cannot resist the temptation to count every last straw on the broom. This is a laborious task and usually lasts until dawn, at which point the hag is no longer powerful or invisible and must go home and get back into her skin. The spirit will burn and then disintegrate if she is unable to slip into her skin before the sun rises.

Other objects that confuse and torture boo hags are brushes, sieves, and strainers. They stop to count the bristles or the holes and lose most of the night doing so.

Unfortunately, some hags have the gift of speedy counting, so other measures must be taken. Painting the exterior doors and window frames in-digo blue wards off evil.

Hags are also believed to be afraid of gunpowder, so those fearing a visit from a boo hag have been known to place a loaded gun under their pillows or by their beds to keep evil spirits away (which is dangerous and not recommended). No one is sure why this works, but apparently it has worked successfully on many occasions.

In the home of someone fearful of the boo hag, you'll also find many candles burning throughout the night and a salt shaker by his or her bedside. The smell of a burning candle keeps the hag away, and some believe that placing a perimeter of salt around the bed will do the same. However, if a hag does show up, salt should be scattered into the air as soon as the air turns hot and moist and begins to smell of rotting meat; a salted hag is unable to get back into her skin. For maximum protection, paint exterior doors and window frames Indigo Blue, hang a strainer on the doorknob or set a broom by the door, burn candles all night, and scatter salt around the bed.

Finally, Gullahs also believe that the right prayer can stop a boo hag.

Amen.

Hound of Goshen

This is a strange and incredible tale about a "plateye," or apparition. The story begins circa 1850, when a horrible murder coincided with the appearance of a traveling salesman and his companion dog. Because the dog was white and very large, with a long snout and big tail, some speculated he was a wolfhound. When the murder occurred, the townspeople blamed the salesman, who was the only outsider in town at the time. It had to be him. After all, if this interloper didn't do it, that meant one of the townspeople committed the crime, and no one wanted to believe that a neighbor or trusted friend was a murderer. It felt safer to assume it was just a stranger passing through.

Although there was no real evidence against him, his accusers argued that he had two strikes against him: no one could vouch for his character and it couldn't be coincidence that he had arrived in town just before a murder occurred. On that logic alone, the man was found guilty and hanged. His poor dog, tied to a nearby tree, howled to wake the dead when the hanging took place, but could not break free from the rope until it was too late to save his owner. When he could, he charged over to the limp body that had been cut down from the noose and lay on the ground beside it. The sheriff raised his rifle ready to shoot the beast, but the dog ran into the woods before the sheriff could take aim.

Sightings of a "ghost dog"—so called because the animal was

not like a normal or "real" dog—began within a few months. His appearance and movements were extraordinary. One minute the giant dog was chasing someone, and the next minute he was several yards in front of the victim!

The dog attacked only those who participated in or witnessed the hanging of his master. One man suffered such a bad bite on his arm that the limb was nearly useless for the rest of his life. Many sightings occurred, but the dog merely chased the person or ran right by him or her. The beast seemed to know exactly whom he was looking for—anyone associated with the hanging was his prey. But the sight of the plateye was enough to scare anyone. That's what the slaves called the animal, a plateye. They believed an evil spirit had taken over the dog's body. The entity was restless and looking to wreck havoc on those who had betrayed his owner.

The first to see the ghost dog was a country doctor, George Douglass, in 1855. It happened on Old Buncombe Road, which ran parallel to Interstate 26. Goshen Township was a village along Old Buncombe Road, which is where both the murder and the subsequent hanging took place. One of William Hardy's slaves was dispatched to Doc Douglass's home one night when another slave became gravely ill. The slave arrived, giving the doctor the message and fulfilling his errand, but also looking done in by the trip. The physician got his coat and bag and headed for the door. The slave did not follow, though, just huddled against the doorway, looking frightened and hesitant. Doc Douglass wondered if he too was ill.

He led the slave to a chair, directed him to sit, and asked how he was feeling. The man replied he was fine, but his voice was shaky. The doctor asked if he was okay to travel. The slave stammered that he "didn't want to go back down dat road where dat spirit dog roam."

Knowing that Gullah slaves were very superstitious, the doctor did not try to talk him out of his beliefs, though of course, the wise old man didn't believe in such nonsense as spirit dogs himself. Instead, he figured the slave had seen a rabid dog or fox or something like that. By pointing out that the patient could not wait until morning and would surely die without getting the proper care and medicine, he finally convinced the young man to head back; the slave did not want that on his conscience, so he summoned his courage and led the way. They did not encounter the dog that night, but Dr. Douglass did see the spirit dog on another night and on a different house call.

Another physician, Dr. Jim Cofield, swore to have seen the hound on many occasions. Usually, the doctor's dog kept him company when he had to travel the dark roads to see patients. Whenever the doctor saw the ghost dog, his own dog would disappear into the woods and would not reappear until his owner had passed the stretch of road the ghost dog haunted.

Dr. Cofield said that he was never afraid of the ghost dog, but many others have been frightened by the encounter. In 1936, Berry Sanders claimed the ghost dog chased him nearly a mile on his way home from work and that he saw the dog run right through a big, closed gate. When Sanders got close to his house, however, the dog turned and trotted off.

In 1967, Jim Garrett had a similar experience while on his way to visit a friend. He ran when the dog began to chase him but stumbled and fell. He passed out. When he awoke he recalled feeling a heavy weight on his back just before he blacked out. He also found blood and shallow bite marks on the back of his shirt and skin.

During the 1970s, a woman who lived on Old Buncombe Road spotted the ghost dog as it entered her front yard. She was sitting on her front porch, enjoying the evening breeze, until she saw the dog running toward the porch. She promptly fainted from fear. When she awoke, the dog was gone, and she never saw it again. But then, she never sat on her porch at night again, either!

The ghost dog is always described as an unusually large, albino-white dog with a long snout and big tail. The five-mile stretch of land where the ghost dog roams is between Maybintor and Goshen Hill in Union County. The ghost dog has been seen as recently as 1998. He is believed to be an omen of death.

About Plateyes

A plateye is an evil entity that takes the form of a big animal, such as a dog, bear, or horse.

How does one know it is a plateye and not a normal animal? A plateye assuming the body of an animal is always much larger than the normal-sized animal and has an eerie, surreal appearance. Some say the animals seem to breathe fire, have an indescribable look in their eye or eyes (some claim a plateye has only one big eye), and are accompanied by strong, foul-smelling odors. Furthermore, they apparently have large fangs and front teeth but no back teeth.

Plateyes especially like the Lowcountry because of its abundance of swamps, agricultural areas, fields, woods, and other less-developed areas.

Plateyes torment some humans either as punishment or because they are directed to do so by a root doctor. Like the boo hag, the plateye has weaknesses. It is fond of whiskey, for instance, so if you come across one, you can just pour a little of the alcohol onto the ground so that the spirit will stop to drink it, giving you time to escape. Keeping a flask on you, then, may be a good idea if you are worried about such an encounter. But not everyone agrees that this is the way to go—some believe the best thing to do if faced with a plateye is to stand your ground and recite the Lord's Prayer.

Why You Shouldn't Mess with Voodoo

I've always been fascinated by black magic and can easily picture conjurers mixing herbs and other weird items to create powerful potions. I must have been about twelve years old when I asked my aunt if we could make a money potion, as I was tired of my meager allowance. My Aunt Dee Dee grabbed me by the arm and practically shook me. She looked me square in the eye and warned me *never* to mess with voodoo. She was from Charleston and her people from way back were all from the Lowcountry, so she knew what she was talking about. She shared a story with me that day, one I have never forgotten.

A young man she had gone to school with had gotten himself in a world of trouble because of a potion when he became infatuated with a girl who did not return his affections. She worked in a dress shop across the street from his employer, and every day he had tortured himself by watching her through the store's big front window.

Convinced he was in love with the girl, he tried everything he could think of to woo her. He brought her lunch a few times, as well as flowers. He tried to walk her home, but she made up excuses; he asked her out on a date, but she politely refused. The more she dismissed him, the crazier it made him. He didn't know what to do to sway her and his heart grew heavier each day.

One night he watched her leave work, smiling as he watched

her lock up the store for the night. She was wearing a new dress and it looked really nice on her. When she turned around, he planned to wave to her. If she waved back, he would go over and ask her out again. As she turned around and he prepared to raise his arm to wave, a man came up behind her and grabbed her! Before he could get out the door to go help her, he saw her kiss this guy. Dumbfounded, he watched as the pair walked arm in arm down the street. They looked like they belonged together.

He knew he had to do something. She had a new suitor, and if he didn't act fast, he would lose her forever. He tossed and turned all that night. Sleep never came, but a plan did—he knew what he had to do.

At sunrise, he set off to find a woman he'd heard was capable of casting special spells and making powerful potions, though she was also said to be half crazy. He got lost a few times, but finally found her place. With all his courage, he knocked on the door of the run-down shack. No one answered. What would he do if she wasn't at home? After pounding on the decrepit wood with his fist for nearly a minute, it was finally yanked open by a ghastly-looking old woman. She wore a long, black dress and matching boots. The ensemble was faded and spooky. Her long, unkempt hair was also black, but streaked with gray. He was assaulted by her smell, a rank combination of liquor and body odor.

"What do you want?" she croaked as she put her face up close to his. He wanted to turn and run away, but his legs wouldn't move.

"I've come to…to buy a love potion," he stammered.

"Bring two bottles of whiskey and come back in three days," she told him. And with that, she slammed the door in his face.

In three days, he again banged on her door. He had changed his mind and decided not to come—until he saw his beloved go to lunch with the fellow from the other night. With that image in mind, he returned, though with great trepidation. The old witch signaled him inside, waving impatiently when he hesitated. After once again gathering his courage, he stepped into what must have been the living room but more closely resembled a laboratory. Strewn about the room were jars filled with insects and spices and who knew what else, as well as stones and candles of various sizes and shapes.

The hag held something out to him. He squinted in the dark room and saw that it was a small vial of yellowish liquid—the love potion! She opened his palm and placed the elixir into it. Then she grabbed the whiskey from him and, after inspecting the bottles, set them on a table.

"Listen carefully!" she warned, and then proceeded to give him explicit instructions as to how to use the potion.

But when the time came, the young man was so nervous and excited he couldn't remember what the hag had told him. He put several drops into a cup of tea and carried it over to the girl, who graciously accepted it. Then, as he left her store, he softly recited the words the witch had told him as best he could remember. He returned to work, but watched the girl through the window. She didn't behave any differently. He continued this ritual for a few days. Since he couldn't remember for how many days the witch had told him to perform the ritual, he did it for five days (he was only supposed to do it for three).

Whatever was in the potion sure worked. When he walked over to her store on the eve of the third day and asked her to dinner, she eagerly accepted. They went out almost every night after that, and at first he was so happy and just couldn't believe his good fortune. But then she began to grate on his nerves. She wanted to be with him all the time, and when they were together, she gushed about how much she loved him and asked him to tell her everything he had done since they had last talked. She was also too jealous—if he so much as said hello or tipped his hat to a woman of any age, she went into a rage. It was too much. He began to dread even the sight of her.

The young man eventually went back to see the voodoo woman, begging her to reverse the spell. She brushed off his pleas, though, telling him, "I warned you to be careful. It cannot be undone."

He went home determined to try to make the relationship work. After all, it had been what he wanted. But the next day as she clung to him and told him how much she had missed him since the day before, he knew he couldn't do it. He tried to be gentle, saying that maybe they were spending too much time together.

"That isn't possible, my love," she replied. "I can't bear for us to be apart for even one moment."

Finally, he broke it off. He said he was sorry, but that he didn't feel the same way. The girl was clearly devastated, wailing and begging him for another chance. "What have I done?" she cried.

"I'm sorry," was all he could think to say before turning to leave.

Before he stepped out the door, she picked up a pair of dress shears and stabbed herself in the heart. "If I can't have you, I do not wish to live," she whispered as she fell to the ground. He rushed over to her, scooped her up in his arms, and raced her down the street to the doctor.

But it was too late. The doctor pronounced her dead and gave the young man a comforting pat on the shoulder. "I'm so sorry, son," the physician said sadly.

The girl was buried two days later, and soon after, mysterious beads of blood began appearing on the young man's hands. He kept washing them, but the spots always came back. The townspeople said he had that poor girl's blood on his hands, for sure, as they all thought he was to blame for her death—he had pursued that sweet girl until he got her and then he changed his mind! Ostracized by everyone in town for what he had done to that girl and because of his creepy blood-stained hands, the young man also lost his job and longtime friends. His last hope was the witch.

Dejectedly, he rode to her shack. But when he got there, the hovel stood bare of furniture and vacant of occupants. The only evidence the hag had ever been there was her lingering odor and some empty whiskey bottles.

Having nowhere to go and no one to go to, he stayed and lived the rest of his days in the dilapidated structure, hidden away from the rest of the world.

The Big, Bad Bugaloo

In this book you'll read tales about haints, hags, plateyes, and conjurers. These are all evil entities. Something that is just as nasty but rarely discussed is the "bugaloo." On moonless nights, a bugaloo may rise from deep in the woods and roam through the Lowcountry looking for victims.

Once upon a time, the meanest man in a St. Helena village brutally attacked a woman. It wasn't the first time the villagers had had problems with him; the man was also believed to be responsible for the death of a dog and had stolen from his neighbors on many occasions. The men from the village got together that same moonless night and decided to teach him a lesson. They took him deep into the woods so that no one would hear him scream. When they started attacking him, they got carried away. After beating him severely, the village men even went so far as to cut off his hands and feet before leaving him tied to a tree to die. The men returned the next day to bury the dead man only to find the man gone! Drops of blood and the ropes used to bind him to the tree were on the ground under the tree, but the man they'd attacked was nowhere to be found. Ever since that night, an evil spirit, which has become known as a bugaloo, goes looking for retribution for what was done to him. So if you're a male in the South Carolina Lowcountry, don't go outside on moonless nights—especially if you are near a heavily wooded area!

If you have to go outside, get yourself a boo-daddy. This is a charm that protects a soul from a bugaloo and is also said to work against a haint, hag, or plateye. A boo-daddy must be created by a knowledgeable conjurer. It is made using plough mud, moss, sweetgrass, and saltwater gathered from just the right places. The mixture is placed inside an amulet or a charm bag and worn for protection.

Haints in the Keyhole House

This story is about a man named George Powell, who outwitted a haint. He had built his first home, a sturdy log cabin that was big and designed to withstand harsh winters, in the woods of western North Carolina. His wife had done her part to make it cozy with pretty curtains and quilts, and the couple was quite happy there until a

mysterious fire destroyed the house late one night. Husband and wife made it outside to safety where they could only watch sadly as their home burned to the ground. The cause of the fire was never found—the stove had not been on and the fire in the fireplace had been nothing but a few smoldering embers, not enough to spark and cause damage. Mr. Powell had seen to that himself before retiring to bed for the night.

But George knew what had happened. A haint had caused the fire! He had heard unexplainable scratching and shuffling on many occasions, including shortly before the fire had begun. Remembering these disturbances, he became convinced that some dratted haint had slipped into the cabin through the front door's tiny keyhole, but had been unable to get out without great difficulty. Like a cat that easily climbs a tree but has trouble getting down from it, it is much easier for a haint to enter a place than to exit. So, as payback for her troubles, the evil spirit had breathed her hot, foul breath as hard as she could into the dying fire, causing flames to rekindle and leap out of the fireplace. The wood structure had surrendered to the hearty fire in no time.

When he built his next home, George kept this experience in mind and altered the design of his house accordingly. For one thing, he used brick, not wood. Also, he incorporated a large keyhole into the front of the house. The odd shape was on the upper part of the brick house, near the master bedroom. No one knows whether it was thanks to these precautions or his moving out of the dense woods where evil spirits were plentiful, but George Powell never again had a problem with haints.

The house he built at 901 Seehorn Street in Lenoir, North Carolina—known as Keyhole House—was eventually torn down and replaced by Trinity United Methodist Church. Before the house was destroyed, however, the keyhole was removed and saved. The bricked-up keyhole can be seen on the sign at the entrance of the old church.

It's important to keep in mind that haints aren't limited to the Lowcountry. They can be found all over the world, wherever forests, swamps, and graveyards are found.

Beware of Haints

Haints or hants are considered by some to be worse than boo hags. A boo hag is a skin-shedding witch (bad enough, I grant you!), but a haint is an angry spirit capable of just as much disturbance. These restless spirits can enter through an opening of any size, from unlocked doors and open windows to decent-sized cracks or holes (such as keyholes). Once inside, they'll start rattling chains or slamming doors or levitating the bed—anything to cause a ruckus and scare the inhabitants. Like boo hags, they don't usually invade until the moon is full. Unlike boo hags, who can be found anywhere, haints prefer graveyards and swamps, so if you live close to a cemetery or dense woods—beware!

A "Jack Mullater" is one type of haint, though it can only be seen when an ideal set of conditions occurs. In swampy areas, there are high concentrations of phosphorescence, which comes from dirt, leaves, fungi, and wood (such as rotten stumps or dead, decaying trees). At night, the phosphorescence glows. In the black night, pierced only by moonlight, the glowing swamp gas is quite an eerie sight. Sometimes, when conditions are just right, this gas will take the form of a translucent ball and float through the air. This usually occurs when there is a nearby road. On a hot day, the road surface remains warm into the evening and the heat from it, mixed with the cool swamp air, causes the phosphorescence to lift up into the atmosphere, creating a loose formation that drifts up and away in the wind. This is when the evil "Jack Mullater" spirit or haint rises up and goes out to make trouble.

Dr. Buzzard, the Most Famous Root Doctor

The most famous root doctor was Dr. Buzzard, aka Stephaney Robinson. He learned his skill from his father, who had learned from a West African medicine man before he was supposedly smuggled from Africa aboard an illegal slave ship. The last known smuggling attempt took place in 1858, but it is possible that his father could have been one of the last groups smuggled into the U.S., as slave trading was still legal in Cuba long after it became illegal here. Or perhaps it was actually his grandfather who was smuggled from Africa and later passed on his skills to him.

Not just anyone can be a witch doctor, also known as a conjurer, sorcerer, or root doctor. You have to have the gift, or "the mantle." This is usually passed down or transferred to a son who has shown he has clairvoyant abilities. On rare occasions, someone with exceptional potential can be apprenticed.

Then again, Dr. Buzzard himself claimed he got his mantle (power) from a mockingbird when it landed on his head—from that moment on, he'd had "the sight."

But whether it came from his father, grandfather, or a bird, folks around St. Helena Island believed he possessed a powerful mantle. For nearly forty years, Dr. Buzzard was sought out for conjuring. He concocted all kinds of potions and often used animals such as cats and snakes in his rituals.

He certainly had a sinister appearance, and perhaps this lent credibility to his claims. He wore loose, black clothing and thick,

blue-purple glasses—day or night. The dark shades guaranteed that no one could look into his eyes. All kinds of folks came to him, including those in trouble with the law, people trying to reach out to deceased relatives, and defendants hoping for a favorable court outcome.

His home, Oaks Plantation, was on the southwest tip of St. Helena Island. Once a week he made a trip inland to the Frogmore Post Office to check his post office box. Every week there were dozens of letters from across the state and from several neighboring states, as well. Most contained cash, checks, or money orders. The shrewd man threw away the payments that required his signature. Root doctoring was illegal because it was practicing medicine without a license. The wily witch doctor wasn't about to get caught in a trap.

People came from near and far begging for Dr. Buzzard to work his magic. His audience increased tenfold as more and more incredible stories circulated. One story involved a Gullah fishing party that drowned. The men had set out in two boats but had met with so much success that the second boat was loaded down with fish, leaving all the men to pile into the smaller boat. On the return trip, there was a terrible storm and the men drowned. Two days later, the boat full of fish arrived at shore with a big buzzard resting atop of the pile of fish. The Gullahs took it as a sign—this was Dr. Buzzard's doing.

While the root doctor had many tricks in his bag, one or two of them were especially strange. Reportedly, Dr. Buzzard had a magical seashell that he said was a direct line to Satan. If someone didn't pay him or tried to cross him, the witch doctor would grab the seashell and call out for Satan to listen to what he wanted the Devil to do to that person.

There is a legend that one of the many times that Dr. Buzzard was arrested or brought in for questioning by the sheriff, Dr. Buzzard told his captors that he had absolute proof he was a bona fide witch doctor. He was no charlatan, he assured the men. To prove his point, he asked that they lock him in a coffin, promising them he could escape. This they had to see, the jailers told him. A coffin was brought to the building and Dr. Buzzard climbed inside. As he lay down, he told them he would be out by the time they finished their lunch.

The coffin was closed and chains were wrapped around it. The locks were secured and double-checked, and then the men walked across the street to eat, laughing at Dr. Buzzard's pledge. When they returned, they found the chains and locks lying on the floor near the coffin. The men opened the coffin, and a black cat jumped out!

A flock of buzzards showed up one day and made their home on top of the Beaufort water tower, which was right behind the Beaufort County Courthouse. When Dr. Buzzard made a court appearance on behalf of a client that same day, the buzzards left their perch and flew around the courthouse several times. The Gullahs took this as a sure sign that Dr. Buzzard's mantle was working perfectly.

To sway the outcome of a trial or court proceeding, Gullah

defendants sometimes hired root doctors to come into court and work their magic, or at least send along a strong root or powder concoction. Dr. Buzzard was inarguably the best root doctor, and if his high fees could be paid, he would come to court and speak in tongues, give the evil eye to adversaries, chew on a root, or do whatever he deemed most effective.

On these occasions, court proceedings were turned topsy-turvy. Imagine the scene: huge, soaring buzzards circling overhead outside the courthouse, the ominous black clothing and creepy glasses worn by the notorious Dr. Buzzard, and his entourage of admirers and curiosity seekers. How intimidating this all must have been to witnesses, jurors, and the opposing counsel! I imagine even the judge himself must have been taken aback.

One person who remained unimpressed with the root doctor was Sheriff J.E. McTeer. He was elected in 1926 and saw many strange things that were attributed to Dr. Buzzard, such as people getting sick and dying or witnesses having seizures in the middle of testifying in court.

Ed McTeer grew up in the Lowcountry, so he was no stranger to this stuff; he knew all about the Gullahs and their beliefs. He learned firsthand from the Gullah men and women who worked on his grandfather's rice plantation and his father's farm, and several of these slaves and their descendants practiced voodoo. Furthermore, his grandmother was a medium for the spirit world, and McTeer recalled witnessing a séance at his grandparent's home when he was a boy. He remembered it so well because the table moved and shook when his grandmother placed her tiny arms and hands on top of it.

The sheriff also believed that he inherited some of his grandmother's gift and began a lifelong study of conjuring so he could better understand it. In time, he became known as a "white root doctor." On one occasion, he answered a call and went into a local honky tonk. The lights went out soon after he entered the premises and then gunfire exploded. Those on the scene swear that the criminal fired shots at the sheriff, yet the man didn't suffer so much as a scratch! This fueled the belief that he was protected by black magic and should be feared. Another time, he was shot at during a burglary in progress but again escaped uninjured! This made him a legend.

McTeer felt strongly that he was the one who could stop Dr. Buzzard once and for all. He devised a plan but before he could carry it out, World War II came to the Lowcountry. Sheriff McTeer was responsible for overseeing beach patrols, and his mind was far from the conjurer until the military kept rejecting the draftees from St. Helena Island.

The draft board sent many Gullah men to Fort Jackson, but the base sent most of the men back home, citing poor health. The military physicians named the condition "hippity-hoppity heart syndrome." It was no freak coincidence that these men shared the same ailments, diarrhea and heart palpitations. McTeer was so sure of this he sent a letter to the U.S. War Department outlining his beliefs and the reasons for them. The government didn't hold much stock in McTeer's claims until a busload of St. Helena recruits became critically ill on their way to Fort Jackson. One man died before reaching the hospital.

An investigation revealed that these men had ingested potions they had purchased for $50 apiece that were guaranteed to make them slightly sick and get them released from military duty. Despite their initial cooperation, none of the young men dared testify against a mighty root doctor, let alone the greatest root doctor, Dr. Buzzard. Sheriff McTeer, with a great deal of persuasion, managed to obtain a small bottle of this potion from one of the sick men. Autopsy results showed that the deceased had ingested a double dose of the potion to be certain he failed his physical and avoided military service. The tests also proved the potion was a mixture of oleander leaves (digitalis), rubbing alcohol, moth balls, and lead. No wonder the young men suffered wild heart palpitations!

The sheriff finally had the witch doctor dead to rights—or so he thought. The pharmacy records proved that another root doctor, Dr. Bug, was the one who had purchased the arsenic and created the lethal tonics. Strangely, Dr. Bug didn't even deny his role in the deception. He was found guilty and forced to pay a hefty fine. Soon thereafter, Dr. Bug took to his bed and died within the year.

Sheriff McTeer, or the "High Sheriff" as some called him, never gave up his campaign to stop Dr. Buzzard. He nearly had the witch doctor when a burglary suspect was apprehended with a root and a bag of white powder. The suspect refused to answer his questions until McTeer went to his desk and put on sinister sunglasses that closely resembled the blue-purple ones worn by Dr. Buzzard. The suspect broke down and confessed everything. Dr. Buzzard had sold him the root to make him invisible and the white powder to prevent his capture.

Despite this knowledge, the case never made it to court. As soon as the witness saw Dr. Buzzard enter the interrogation room, he started shaking, fell to the floor, and began rolling around violently. The sheriff knew the poor man would never be able to testify against the root doctor, so he dismissed the charges against the conjurer. However, Sheriff McTeer issued a warning that if the witch doctor didn't stop, he would eventually bring him to justice.

The infamous root doctor was not used to being threatened. To the contrary—most folks feared or respected him too much to even think about it. The sheriff's warning made him so mad that the witch doctor set out to ruin him. The spiritual warfare came to a halt after Dr. Buzzard's son was killed in a car crash. The conjurer believed the wreck was the High Sheriff's doing and went to see his adversary. The root doctor told the sheriff that he respected his mantle and would leave him alone if McTeer would do the same. McTeer agreed, on the condition that Dr. Buzzard quit practicing sorcery. The conjurer thought about it for several seconds before nodding his head in agreement.

Dr. Buzzard was later caught root doctoring, despite his promise to McTeer. He hired a white lawyer to defend him when he was arrested, but was found guilty and ordered to pay a fine. He died a few months later, in 1947, of stomach cancer. But there may have still been a powerful root doctor, the High Sheriff, practicing black magic.

At the next election, a former highway patrolman challenged McTeer. The candidate put on an aggressive campaign and there was mud-slinging on both sides. The race was so tight that televised speeches were scheduled. After McTeer gave his speech, it was the other man's turn. But when he began to speak, all the TVs in the area succumbed to static interference.

Nonetheless, the challenger won by a narrow margin. But his term was tumultuous, ending with the assault of a grand jury foreman, who just happened to be a retired brigadier general. The sheriff fled the courtroom, locked himself in his house, and threatened suicide. Officials managed to get him out of the house and into counseling. Many locals believed this was the work of J.E. McTeer.

McTeer eventually wrote a book, *Fifty Years as a Lowcountry Witch Doctor*. When he died in 1976, his son became the only white root doctor in Beaufort County. Dr. Buzzard's surviving son, Buzzy, was also a root doctor until his death in 1997.

The whereabouts of Dr. Buzzard's grave remain a secret. There is an unmarked gravesite in a Baptist church cemetery on St. Helena Island that some believe belongs to him. However, some swear he was never buried at all and that upon his death, his body parts were used by other root doctors for special conjuring.

Why Root Doctors Wear Shades

Root doctoring is just another form of conjuring. It is a combination of knowledge passed on and a gift for clairvoyance. The knowledge involves learning how to make charms and potions using herbs, and also the rituals that will ensure they work.

Root doctors were tolerated during the days of slavery because traditional treatments and cures were poor, to say the least. And actually, Confederate Army surgeon Francis Porcher asked root doctors and Indians for herbal remedies when Charleston's supply lines were damaged during the Civil War.

With the advances of modern medicine, the herbal remedies provided by root doctors are frowned upon nowadays. While there are stores that still carry these products, the labels do not guarantee success but rather are clearly marked with words such as "may" and "alleged."

The prescribed root may or may not contain herbs. The root may be a charm or mojo that is chewed, worn, or buried, depending on the doctor's instructions.

The most common charms sought after are love charms, money charms, power charms, and health charms.

Just as important as the ingredients used in the charms are the rituals performed by the root doctor. The words spoken and actions taken by the root doctor while making the charm are never revealed.

We do, however, know some of the popular ingredients found in these charms. Goofer dust is graveyard dust that, if being used to make a root for a good luck charm, is gathered just before midnight from the grave of a righteous Christian. If a bad charm is desired, on the other hand, the goofer dust should be gathered just after midnight from the grave of a lost soul. The term "goofer" comes from the African word "kuwfa," meaning "dead person." With either charm in mind, a coin is left on the grave when dirt is removed so as not to offend the deceased. If the spirit becomes offended, he or she may rise up and follow the person home.

Other common ingredients include: herbs, sulphur, salt, asafetida, gunpowder, candle wax, incense, crow feathers, salamander feet, and animal parts (for bad charms). Specific spells and charms are included in the Special Spells chapter .

Root doctors can also give the "evil eye." This is when a spell is cast using a mean look, signs, and chants in tongues. If a conjurer gives the evil eye while chewing on a bad (evil) root, the result is even worse for the intended. Only a powerful conjurer is able to give the evil eye. One long look from him or her could cause unexplainable convulsions, seizures, trembling, or other ailments. This also applies to animals and crops, and stems from an old belief that eyes possess energy, either good or bad. Dr. Buzzard was said to have the gift of the evil eye, which is presumably why he wore the dark purple-blue sunglasses most of the time. It was believed that his mantle was so powerful he could give the evil eye right through those thick glasses. Some fainted with fear when his head turned in their direction.

Root doctors are often named after animals, such as Dr. Buzzard, Dr. Bug, Dr. Fly, Dr. Crow, Dr. Snake, and Dr. Turtle.

Doctor to the Dead

There's a story in a great old book, *The Doctor to the Dead: Grotesque Legends and Folk Tales of Old Charleston,* that is worth sharing. I have rewritten it in my own words to make it easier to understand.

A mean man named Frank "Rumpetty Dick" Middleton got into a fight one day and killed two other bad guys, Meat-Skin Martin and Jorico Pope. Rumpetty Dick was arrested for their murders. It was pretty much an open-and-shut case. After all, there had been lots of witnesses present when the murders took place. It was evident that Rumpetty Dick would be convicted. In desperation, he contacted a local conjurer, Hot-Bread-Cut Jack Warren, and asked the man to help him.

The root doctor promised his assistance. He said, however, that he was not sure what could be done. Warren said it would be hard to defeat the judge, jury, court, sheriff, and God. No, he did not believe he could change the outcome of the trial, but he could try to help. Rumpetty Dick was baffled by the conjurer's words, but he chose to believe it would be all right.

The first day of the trial, a terrible odor permeated the courtroom. It was worse than any smell imaginable. All the witnesses got sick from the awful odor and were unable to testify. Proceedings continued the next day, but the witnesses all took ill again. It was not clear what was wrong with them. Jorico Pope's half-brother had some kind of seizure. The others became disoriented and distraught to the point that either they could not testify at all or their testimony was so garbled that it was not taken seriously. Many believed the strange illness was the result of a powerful charm and evil eye used by the root doctor, who sat in the courtroom watching the witnesses without ever taking his eyes off of them.

Despite the lack of credible testimony, the man was found guilty. He was sentenced to death. Rumpetty Dick cried out in anguish over the outcome. He turned pleadingly to the conjurer, who assured him all was not lost. The morning of his hanging, the conjurer brought him a new pair of socks and an old pair of shoes. He instructed Rumpetty Dick to wear them for the execution.

Rumpetty Dick was transported to the gallows and then led to the right spot, just above the trap door. The rope was placed around his neck. He said a silent prayer as the noose tightened around his neck. This was it! He took a deep breath—but nothing happened! He was still alive! The trap door seemed to be jammed. The hangman threw the lever once again, to no avail. Rumpetty Dick was led off the scaffold while the sheriff and his men fixed the problem. "The third time's the charm," someone joked as he was led back up onto the platform. Then the hangman threw the switch, the trap door opened, and he quickly blacked out.

He awoke on the ground next to the gallows. Wait a minute! He was alive! He reached up and felt his neck. Glory be! The rope had broken before his neck could be snapped.

"Again?" asked the hangman.

"No. This man done be hanged two times. We can't hang him again. The law only allows a man to be hanged once! Let him go," said the sheriff.

The hanging failed, but it did do some damage. His neck was wrung so harshly by the rope before it broke that Rumpetty Dick could no longer hold his head up straight. It tilted to one side, nearly lying on his shoulder. From then on, he had a new nickname. He was known as Crook-Neck Dick!

Do You Believe?

What makes conjuring work is the belief that it works. It's a classic example of the power of suggestion, or "auto-suggestion." I once heard a story about a Gullah man who told his wife he was going to leave her. Laughingly, he told her that he'd found a better woman. Prepared for this proclamation since everyone in town knew by then that he had taken up with this promiscuous woman, the wife had already visited a local root doctor. As her husband prepared to leave, she emptied the packet of sprinkling powder the conjurer had given her into his underwear drawer, dumping all the underwear into the wood-burning stove. She was the one laughing as she watched the garments disintegrate. She turned to her no-good husband, still laughing, and announced he could leave but he wouldn't be getting any satisfaction elsewhere! She told him about her visit to the conjurer and described the charm she had used on him. She smiled as she said his manhood would shrivel up and disappear just as his underwear had in the fire. The man ran from the house at his wife's prediction. It didn't matter what the conjurer had concocted—the man was ruined by the very suggestion of it. He was never able to have sex again, so his mistress left him. He later tried to reconcile with his wife, but she told him she didn't want a half-man. Eventually, he killed himself.

The Apothecary's Folly

In spring of 1867, a young doctor arrived in Charleston. As he walked through the busy streets of the port city, he smiled. It was a bustling town with a fast-growing population. The Civil War had been over for two years and things were changing for the better. This was the place to be for an ambitious man ready to settle down and make his fortune.

However, Dr. Trott soon found out he couldn't afford to open his shop where he had hoped. The cost was too high. So he settled for a less desirable location, content in the knowledge that business would be so good that he'd soon be able to relocate. As he counted his meager monies, he knew it *had* to be soon—his cash had been nearly depleted after buying inventory and supplies.

He put a sign in the window announcing that the store would OPEN SOON. Then he set about getting the place ready for its debut. Trott was so excited about the prospect that he barely slept the night before he was going to open the store. He, who came from such humble beginnings, owned his very own business!

The next morning, he whistled as he strolled down the street from the boarding house to the shop. He paused to admire the APOTHECARY SHOP sign that hung over the door. He took the handmade sign that he had set in the window and crossed out SOON so that the sign now read, OPEN. He hurried behind the counter and waited. And waited. And waited. He looked at his watch and then gasped in horror. It had been nearly three hours since he had opened the shop, and not a single customer!

He ran to the window and peered out into the street. There were dozens of people and wagons along the street. The men and women were shopping in area stores, just not in his store. Maybe they didn't realize he was now open. He made a bigger OPEN sign and placed it in the window. He jerked open the door and hurried outside to look. Certainly no one could miss that sign! He went back inside and resumed his place at the counter. The day dragged on endlessly. Finally, at 6 o'clock that evening, he flipped the OPEN sign over so that the back of it, CLOSED, could be seen. He locked the door and dejectedly returned to his room.

He tried to reassure himself during that sleepless night. It was only the first day, for goodness' sake! He just needed to give it a little more time. Folks needed medicines, so sooner or later they would come. But they didn't. Three days came and went and the only customer he had was a woman who bought some headache relief. She had told him that most folks in this part of Charleston didn't have money to buy remedies or, even if they did, tended to rely on root doctors. They weren't the kind to frequent an apothecary shop.

Trott was demoralized when she left. He hadn't even considered that he would be competing with conjurers! Why, they were nothing more than charlatans. He had a great deal of time to think about his situation during the long, dull days that followed, so he tried to come up with a plan. What he needed was something that would get people to come into the store. He was confident he could sell them the remedies and other items he stocked if only he could get them inside; to do that, he needed something that most folks would find irresistibly fascinating. And then it hit him. He didn't know what made him think of it, but he was sure it would work. It was something he had seen up north one time when visiting a traveling carnival.

He counted his remaining money, locked up the shop, and went down the street to get the materials he would need. He decided to keep the shop closed for business until he was ready to put his plan in motion. Glass he'd ordered for the project was delivered the next morning. He hung the sign he made across the outside of the store over the large window so that no one could see inside. The new sign read, FREE MAGIC SHOW IN FOUR DAYS. He cleaned out the little storeroom above the shop and proceeded with his plan. Each morning he changed the sign, FREE MAGIC SHOW IN THREE DAYS, FREE MAGIC SHOW IN TWO DAYS, and then, finally, FREE MAGIC SHOW TOMORROW. He noticed many people watching him as he changed his sign each day. He also caught folks trying to peek in the window or even the door as workmen entered or exited. He smiled in satisfaction. That last day before his event, he walked all around Charleston passing out flyers he'd made announcing this special "once in a lifetime" show.

When Trott got to the store the next morning, there was already

a large crowd waiting! Judging by their fancy clothes, people had come from King Street and beyond. Word had sure spread like wildfire. The sight of all those high-class folks coming all the way to the Bottle Alley area then drew curious locals to the shop. They figured that if the rich white folk thought it worthwhile, maybe there was something to the place. After all, these people didn't tend to visit this part of town, so this must be big.

It had taken every bit of his money to transform the shop, but it looked like it was going to be worth it. He let as many as would fit into his shop, telling them to look around while he prepared for the show. He took the steps two at a time and went on to set everything up. Once he was ready, Trott began to lead the eager people upstairs. They found it full of ocean exhibits. Fancy glass tanks, which people tentatively touched and then looked inside of, were placed all around the room. Some of the tanks held unusual shells and reptiles. Others were full of water and colorful fish and turtles! Folks had never seen anything like this before. There were no aquariums back then, when fish were only seen in the river or on a dinner plate. He didn't tell the crowd, but he had spent days on the waterway to find all the things that he had on display. He had gone all the way to Savannah to get the glass tanks.

After allowing his guests a few minutes of appreciative speculation, Trott led the group to the dimly lit back of the room. He told them that what they had seen was just the preview for the real show. He cleared his throat before dramatically announcing that they were going to have a chance to see something that mere mortals had never seen before—a real, live mermaid! And with that, he whipped the sheet off to reveal a huge tank filled with fish that were even bigger and prettier than those in the small tanks. Something that looked like the tail of a mermaid could be seen swimming behind a large plant. The water was murkier than the other tanks and there were more fish, plants, and shells, so it was hard to be sure.

But one man yelled out: "I seen her! I seen the mermaid! She's a beauty." And then everyone began to claim they had too. At this, Dr. Trott threw the cover back over the huge aquarium and hustled the group back downstairs. As the would-be customers protested, he explained that there were many others waiting. He suggested they browse around the store and said maybe they could try again later.

By the time he got downstairs, there was a line waiting to buy items people had picked up while waiting for the free show. He took care of them as quickly as possible, but it still took a while. Those waiting to go upstairs grew impatient. Most stayed, but a few left, saying they would try later. A local conjurer watched the crowd from across the street. She shook her head as she shuffled away.

Realizing he needed help, Trott asked the lady who ran the boarding house if she could recommend someone to assist him in his shop. She suggested her son, Joe, promising the boy was trustworthy and hardworking. After some discussion to make sure the lad understood what was expected of him, Trott decided to give him a chance. Joe was ready and waiting when he came down for breakfast the next day. On their way to the store, Trott explained that he would take care of the shop while Joe led the "tours" upstairs. He cautioned that the boy needed to limit the groups to no more than six people.

"Why only six?" Joe asked.

"I don't want too many folks going through too quickly. They need enough time in the store to decide to buy something!" he said. He also warned Joe to only give them a minute or so to look at the mermaid tank before escorting them out. He knew he'd hired the right person for the job when the young man suggested they charge ten cents per person to see the show.

People eagerly plucked down the money to go upstairs. This plan worked well for several days, until a terrible storm hit Charleston. This was no normal storm. It was a wicked hurricane that caused massive flooding and damage. Even after the hurricane had passed, the rain didn't stop. Homes and businesses were washed away. The roof of the apothecary shop was damaged by the storm and had begun leaking badly in a few spots. The owner, Trott's landlord, promised to address the matter as soon as the rain stopped. But when would that happen? It had already been eight days of nonstop rain. Folks were getting stir-crazy. And then things got really bad.

The local conjurer woman claimed the rain would not stop until the captured mermaid was returned to the sea. She said she'd had visions and knew for certain this was true. It would only get worse, she warned, if the mermaid was not freed. At first, most people laughed at this prophecy. But then more and more homes and businesses and livestock were lost to the flooding. The conjurer continued her doom and gloom prophesizing and people began to listen. When a boy drowned in the river trying to save his dog, the locals decided to take action. Enough was enough!

An angry crowd of citizens stormed the apothecary shop. They demanded the mermaid. Trott tried to calm them, but to no avail. He told them that the conjurer had only said that about the mermaid because she wanted to drive him out of business. Folks were coming to him for cures instead of her and she was desperate to get rid of him. Finally, he confessed there was no mermaid. He said it was all a trick. No one believed him. He told them to come upstairs and he would show them. The group rushed upstairs, nearly running over Dr. Trott. As the group started across the room toward the large tank in the rear, the roof collapsed! When the heavy debris hit the aquariums, it broke the glass. All the fish spilled out onto the floor. Torrents of rain poured into the room now that the roof was gone. The rush of water broke through one of the building's thin walls, pushing the contents of the tanks outside. Everyone grabbed onto posts or railings to prevent being carried out by the surge of water.

The rain stopped about an hour later. When the chaos ended, the crowd looked for the apothecary man, but he was never found! Nor was the mermaid. The conjurer said the mermaid had swum back to sea, taking the apothecary with her as punishment for capturing her. Others wondered if there ever really was a mermaid.

His assistant, Joe, swore there had been. He said that his employer had hired a root doctor (but would not disclose the man's name for fear of reprisal) to help him obtain the creature. Joe wasn't sure whether the root doctor had created the concoction or whether he'd merely dispensed advice that was then used by the apothecary, but Joe swore some kind of sprinkling powder had been made and used to shrink her to half her normal size. He had seen her with his own eyes and assured everyone that she was as real as you or me!

About Apothecaries

Back before there were big chain drugstores such as Walgreens and CVS, there were apothecary shops. In addition to herbal and chemical remedies, these pharmacies sold tobacco and other merchandise. Medical advice was also given and minor procedures sometimes performed. Eventually, soda fountains could be found inside most shops.

There are two great places in the eastern U.S. to learn about apothecaries:

The Stabler-Leadbeater Apothecary Museum was founded in 1732 by Edward Stabler as an apothecary shop. It operated until 1933, when the Great Depression caused it to close. It reopened in 1939 as the museum it remains today. Visitors will enjoy a short film and find two floors of exhibits filled with more than 8,000 items. The museum is located at Stabler's Old Stand, 105-107 South Fairfax Street, Alexandria (Old Town), VA 22314. (703) 838-3852. www.apothecarymuseum.org

The New Orleans Pharmacy Museum was once a pharmacy or apothecary founded by America's first licensed pharmacist, Louis J. Dufilho Jr. Up until 1804, a person could apprentice in a shop for six months and then make and sell any and all medications to the public. Customers often got the wrong medications and doses. A law was passed in Louisiana in 1804 that required a license to operate a pharmacy. Pharmacists had to pass a three-hour exam given by a panel of reputable doctors and pharmacists. Dufilho was the first person to pass the exam in 1816. He opened his shop in 1823, which later became the New Orleans Pharmacy Museum. It is on Chartres Street in the French Quarter, New Orleans, LA 70130. (504) 565-8027. www.pharmacymuseum.org.

Most folks don't realize this, but apothecaries once sold voodoo items such as love potions, sprinkling powders, herbal remedies, cachets, and more.

Mermaid or Hoax?

Was there a real mermaid, or was this a hoax? Many believe it was a big hoax. If so, the doctor may have gotten the mermaid idea from P. T. Barnum, who came up with his famous Fiji mermaid hoax in 1842. The mermaid he displayed was supposedly captured in the South Pacific Fiji islands by a naturalist. However, Barnum had hired a man he called Dr. Griffin to pretend to be an accredited naturalist who had authenticated the "Feejee Mermaid." The mermaid was shown to sold-out crowds in New York (where Dr. Trott was originally from and where he may have learned about the mermaid) and Boston. The creature eventually disappeared, and no one knows what happened to it. The shriveled mermaid he possessed is believed by some to have been created using half a fish for the lower body and half a monkey or ape for the upper body. This type of curiosity can still be seen in some circus sideshows. We'll never know the truth about this particular story, since the "mermaid" and Dr. Trott disappeared during the storm, but we do know that the conjurer who was responsible for shutting down the apothecary shop had more customers than ever once Dr. Trott was gone! Perhaps the conjurer performed a "Get Rid of Someone" charm or spell.

Kingdom of Oyotunji:
Voodoo Village

Bet you didn't know that we had an African country (depending on whom you ask) smack in the middle of South Carolina's Lowcountry! The Kingdom of Oyotunji is an African village located in Sheldon, South Carolina, in Beaufort County. "Oyotunji" means "to rise again." The "kingdom" was founded by the late Oba Efuntola (sometimes also spelled as Ofuntola) Oseijeman Adelabu Adefunmi I in 1970 to represent a Nigerian Yoruba village. It is an independent nation and there is a sign at the entrance that reads, "You are now leaving the United States."

No one is sure why King Oba wanted to start an authentic African village/country in America. Some accounts say he was a fugitive from the law, while others say he did it so that he could not be governed by our laws. The Kingdom of Oyotunji is not a part of the United States, according to the king's accountants. (I assume that they pay taxes or have a religious tax exemption; if not, the king would have been arrested and the land seized long ago!) Residents do pay rent and taxes to the kingdom, and they have utilities and phones. They sell handmade items to earn money to pay these expenses. Reportedly, at one time religious rites and root doctoring were done for a fee. It has been nicknamed the "Voodoo Village" by some.

King Oba was formerly Walter Eugene King from Detroit. He was once a dancer who performed throughout the U.S., Europe, Asia, Africa, and Haiti as a member of the Katherine Dunham Dance Company. After becoming fascinated with Haitian and African religious beliefs, he traveled to Cuba in 1959 to become a Yoruba priest. He changed his name to Oba Efuntola Oseijeman Adelabu Adefunmi and, in 1970, bought property in Beaufort County that became the Kingdom of Oyotunji. In 1972, he went to Nigeria to get initiated into the Ifa priesthood so that he could become King Oba.

The Yoruba religion began in Africa, specifically in Nigeria and the Republic of Benin. Yorubas were taken as slaves (just like the Gullahs) to Cuba and America. However, that is where their similarities to the Gullahs end. As part of their religion, the Yorubas practice animal sacrifice, polygamy, and divination.

In other parts of the world, the core principles of Yoruba have been incorporated into other religions, therefore becoming known by other names. In Cuba, Yoruba is called "Santería" or "Lukumí," and in America, "Oyotunji" (hence, the name Kingdom of Oyotunji). Arguably, it is the largest African-originated religion in the world. There are many similarities between vodou (Haitian voodoo) and Yoruba, especially for those that consider voodoo a religion. They share many common beliefs and traditions. The basic philosophy of Yoruba is that all human beings have a Manifest Destiny (they call it "Ayanmo") to become one in spirit with our creator (who is known as "Olódùmarè"). Every thought and action done by human beings impacts all other living things on Earth. So, the idea is that your destiny is in your hands by the way you think and live. If you're living right, you are moving toward your Ayanmo.

People began to flock to this kingdom, where citizens farmed to survive and had no electricity or running water. In the late '70s and early '80s, the population was as many as 250. The heat, insects, and lack of amenities drove many away, however, and these days the kingdom is rumored to house no more than ten or twelve families. And while the communal living concept remains, little farming is done these days. It will be interesting to see if this isolated kingdom can endure. A similar establishment, the Nuwaubian Pyramids community in neighboring Georgia, did not survive. The Oyotunji villagers are confident their way of life will remain intact. They claim there are as many as four hundred people in the area who practice

Yoruba but choose not to live in the village proper.

King Obu "passed" on February 3, 2005. According to the Yoruba religion, he is not dead but instead has "gone up the ceiling."

The beliefs held by this sect are based on the ancient African Yoruba religion. When he was alive, the king appeared on the Oprah Winfrey Show to discuss his people's custom of polygamy. He had as many as fourteen wives, twenty-two children, and twenty-three grandchildren. His grandson, Adelabu Adefunmi II, became the new king in July 2005.

The U.S. "kingdom" was built in the midst of a South Carolina forest. There are winding dirt roads and primitive edifices, including homes, a royal palace, monuments, temples, and mausoleums. A hand-painted sign outside its entrance tells us the road going into Oyotunji is "Safari Road."

It is believed that this South Carolina sanctuary closely resembles its counterparts in Africa. There is a shrine of sorts to each of the Yoruba deities. Each shrine has a priest who is responsible for its maintenance and for performing pertinent rituals. The village revolves around a calendar of spiritual activities. On the first day of the new year, a reading of the year is done during a ceremony led by the village priests. Many festivals are held throughout the year, such as the Olokun Festival, where they celebrate Yemoja, priestess of the sea. The festival thanks her for her blessings in anticipation of the upcoming planting season.

While it is private, the Oyotunji African Village is sometimes open to visitors. You should call to verify this and inquire about entrance fees before going.

The village is located about fourteen miles north of Beaufort, just south of Yemassee, near Sheldon. Take the I-95 exit for US 17. Drive east for 1.5 miles, then bear right on Trask Parkway (US17/21). After about three miles, you should spot Bryant Lane/Safari Road on the left. You can't miss it! For more information, call (843) 846-8900, or go to www.oyotunjiafricanvillage.org.

Glossary

Definitions

Altar: a place set up to perform rituals using charms and/ or voodoo dolls

Anointing oil: It's believed that certain odors have favorable effects on people. So, if you wear a love potion, you cause someone to fall in love with you.

Bateau: a traditional handmade Geechee boat

Beenyahs: folks born on the island (locals)

Blue root: This is the worst kind of charm. The blue root can cause terrible things, such as the inability of chickens to lay eggs or cows to produce milk, droughts, physical and mental sickness, and death.

Max Beauvoir is the son of a doctor who left Haiti in the 1950s to attend City College of New York. He studied chemistry there, and then went on to take graduate studies in biochemistry at the Sorbonne. He returned to Haiti in the 1970s. His grandfather's dying wish was that Beauvoir take over his job as voodoo priest. (See "Houngan.")

Boo hags: Bad spirit that uses witchcraft to get a person to do what she wishes

Comeyahs: folks from across the water (those newer to the area)

Coming tru: the completion of the process of seeking salvation for one's soul

Conjurer: To conjure means "to effect magic." A Gullah conjurer performs black magic. A root doctor or a witch doctor is a conjurer.

Geechee: Geechee is another word for Gullah that is used mainly in Georgia (while Gullah is used in South Carolina). Gullah-Geechee or Saltwater Geechee may also be used to describe people from this region.

Grannies: community healers who use herbal medicine (not to be mistaken for root doctors)

Gris-gris [bag]: A gris-gris bag is a charm created using a variety of ingredients, such as herbs, roots, stones, powders, bones, feathers, and personal items. The same charm can also be made using these items plus oil, which would then be put into a vial instead of bag.

Hant or haint: an angry dead spirit who haunts the living

Hoodoo: a powerful blend of European, American Indian, and African magic rooted in voodoo. This is the actual name for what the Gullah practice. Also known as Lowcountry voodoo.

Houngan: A houngan is a voodoo priest or priestess who operates semi-independently, catering to his or her followers without much structure (there is no formal hierarchy), although there is now a federation to which many belong. The current leader or spokesman is Max Beauvoir. (www.vodou.org) According to some, houngans steal the souls of dead people, making them zombies who carry out whatever the houngan wants.

Loa: God

Magick (Old English spelling): There are two kinds—white (harmless or benevolent) and black (evil or bad) magic.

Mantle: This is the power and skill of a root doctor, who must get the mantle from some other source, such as a mentor/teacher or animal. A father often passes his gift on to a son. This transference of power is known as passing the mantle.

> The most famous voodoo priestess was Marie Laveau of New Orleans. Her powers were well known during the Civil War. On St. John's Eve (the most sacred of all voodoo celebrations) she would go deep into the bayou around Lake Pontchartrain and perform a ritual to wake the zombies. It included this incantation:
>
> *L'Appe vinie, li Grand Zombi.*
> *L'Appe vinie, pour fe gris-gris."*
> *(He is coming, the great Zombi. / He is coming to make gris-gris.)*

Plateye: A plateye is an evil entity that takes the form of a big animal, such as a dog, bear, or horse. Plateyes torment some humans either as punishment or as directed to do so by a root doctor.

Presider: ward (like a bishop, and highly respected)

Seeking: when a person is involved in the process of seeking salvation for his or her soul

Shape-shifter: another name for a boo hag or witch

Sprinkling powder: This can be made and used in gris-gris bags, sprinkled on a person, or sprinkled around a house (or altar) for protection or additional help.

Vodou: a form of voodoo practiced in the Caribbean (especially Haiti) and in New Orleans

What's in a Name?

Choosing a name for a child is no small task for the Gullah. First, there have to be two names: one public and one private. The private given name is a secret, known only by family. This is to protect the person from harmful magic. It is common for Gullahs to be named according to the month or day of the week of his or her birth, or for personal characteristics. For example, "Anyika" means beauty. The name can also be based on a desired quality, such as hope, or can be inspired by people of importance or supernatural beings.

Voodoo: also known as Santería, ubia, black magic, or simply "the root" by Gullahs

Zombie: corpse revived by voodoo that does whatever the conjurer commands

Some Gullah Words and Phrases

Linguists call the Gullah language an English-based Creole language. This means it is a hybrid language of West African dialects mixed with English, due to the influence of British slave traders and plantation owners. The tale of the "Boo Hag Bride" is partially written in Gullah, so you may find this vocabulary list helpful.

A'min: amen

Beefu't: Beaufort

B'fo' day clean: before dawn

Billige: village

B'leew: believe

Bukrah/buckruh: whites or white people

Buzzut: buzzard

Cawpse: corpse

Chaa'stun: Charleston

Chu'ch: church

Clean skin: a person with light skin

Croaker sack: burlap bag

Crookety: crooked

Daa'k: dark

Dainjus: dangerous

Dark the light: sunset

Dash away: to get rid of a bad habit

Dat: that

Dayclean: dawn

Dem: them

De't': death

Differ: a quarrel

Don' pit mout' on me: don't give me bad luck

'E: pronoun for he, she, it

'E bad mout' me : he cursed me

Ebbuhlastin': everlasting

'E done fuh: he isn't any good (a bad or lazy man)

Eh: yes

'F'aid: afraid

Famemba: remember

Fiah: fire

Flun'rul: funeral

F'o': before

Grabe: grave

Hebby: heavy

Hot the water: bring water to a boil

Hudu: to bring someone bad luck

'Jeckshun: objection

Jedsus: Jesus

Jinnywerry: January

Lub: love, loved, loving; like, liked, liking

Mek so?: Why?

Middleday: noon

Middlenight: midnight

Mo'nuh: mourner

Moobe: move, moved, moving

Nebbuh: never

Nemmin': Never mind

Newnited State: United States

Nowembuh: November

Nyankee: yankee

Oagly: ugly

Ooman: woman

Out the light: turn the light out

Pizen: poison, poisoned, poisoning

Pull off my hat: I had to run

Punkin: pumpkin

Ribbuh: river

Sabeyuh: the Savior

Sa'leenuh: St. Helena Island

Skay'd: scared

Slabe: slave

'Spute: dispute, disputed, disputing

Study yuh head: think hard for the answer

Sweetmouth: flatter

T'engk Gawd: thank God

This side: this island

Tuhbackuh: tobacco

Tuk: took

Washup: worship

Wish de time uh day: pass the time of day (greeting)

Yistiddy: yesterday

"Mus tek cyear a de root fa heal de tree." —Gullah proverb
(Translation: You need to take care of the root in order to heal the tree.)

The Lord's Prayer

Translated to Gullah by Alphonso Brown, as featured on his Gullah Tours website: www.gullahtours.com

Our Fadduh awt'n Hebb'n, all-duh-weh be dy holy 'n uh rightschus name. Dy kingdom com. Oh lawd leh yo' holy 'n rightschus woud be done, on dis ert' as-'e tis dun een yo' grayt Hebb'n. 'N ghee we oh Lawd dis day our day-ly bread. ['N] f'gib we oh Lawd our truspasses, as we also f'gib doohs who com' sin 'n truspass uhghens us. 'N need-us-snot oh konkuhrin' King een tuh no moh ting like uh sin 'n eeb'l. Fuh dyne oh dyne is duh kingdom, 'n duh kingdom prommus fuh be we ebbuh las'n glory. Amen.

Saving Gullah Culture

The Gullahs remained isolated until the 1920s, when the first bridges were built adjoining their sea islands to the mainland. World War II interrupted further progress. It wasn't until the late 1950s that development really began to occur. Now that the Gullahs are no longer isolated, many wonder what the future holds for them. Most continue to live on these islands and nearby communities, making a living fishing, farming, working at resorts, and selling handmade specialty products to tourists who pay top dollar for them. Unfortunately, the astronomical property values driven by championship golf courses, gated communities, and deluxe condos have made it hard for many to afford the increased taxes. Land is selling at more than ten times what it did roughly a decade ago. Oceanfront or waterfront acreage sells for an even higher price.

Some of the younger generation have moved away to find better jobs or go to college, with no plans to return. Both the Gullah and others recognize that something must be done. There are thousands of Gullahs living on St. Helena Island. They have bought and maintained ownership of ninety-percent of the island. They didn't want to see it become another St. Simons or Hilton Head. Additionally, the Gullahs have organized periodic trips to West Africa so that they don't forget their heritage. In an effort to preserve this distinct culture, the Gullah/Geechee Cultural Preservation Act was passed in 2006. Furthermore, Gullah tours, annual festivals and events, and books written on the subject help keep their culture strong.

Resources

Places of Interest

In 2004, the National Trust for Historic Preservation named the Gullah/Geechee Coast as one of America's Most Endangered Historic Places. The Gullah/Geechee Cultural Heritage Act recognizes the **Gullah/Geechee Cultural Heritage Corridor** stretching from Wilmington, North Carolina, to Jacksonville, Florida. It also provides funding and creates a commission to manage the corridor. This will include one or more interpretive centers along the corridor within the next ten years.

African American Heritage Trails. Two trails or routes are offered that offer us glimpses into the history of the African American heritage in South Carolina's Lowcountry. These routes include related businesses (galleries, museums, dining, and more), such as Gullah Cuisine, 1717 Hwy 17 North, Mt. Pleasant, SC 29464; (843) 881-9076 or www.gullahcuisine.com. This restaurant offers Gullah specialties, including gumbo, red rice, collards, and Hoppin' John.

The **African American Coastal Trail** starts at McClellanville and ends just past Edisto Island. Sights include Hampton Plantation State Historic Site, Boone Hall Plantation, Charles Pinckney National Historic Site, Fort Moultrie, Fort Sumter National Monument, Avery Research Center for African American History and Culture, Emanuel AME Church, Old Slave Mart Museum, Aiken-Rhett House, Denmark Vesey House (private), McLeod Plantation, Zion Baptist Church, Hebron Presbyterian Church (where the first African American was trained as a missionary), and the site of the Stono River slave rebellion of 1739.

The **Folkways and Communities Trail** picks up where the African American Coastal Trail ends and extends to north Charleston. You'll see the historic town of Walterboro, St. Peter's AME Church, Tuskegee Airmen Monument, South Carolina Artisans Center, Shady Grove Campground, Summerville-Dorchester Museum, St. Stephens Reformed Episcopal Church, Hillcrest Cemetery, Summerville, Middleton Place, Magnolia Plantation and Gardens, Drayton Hall, Charles Towne Landing, Lincolnville, and Liberty Hill.

For more information: www.sciway.net

About Sea Island Cotton

Many slaves were needed to harvest this crop. The entire Charleston area grew and flourished thanks to Sea Island cotton, which made planters very wealthy and was the most important crop from the late 1700s to the early 1900s. Reportedly, it was never sold at market because the special cotton blend was so highly sought that French mills contracted it practically before it was planted.

Avery Research Center for African American History and Culture has extensive research information available, as well as exhibits and tours. College of Charleston, 125 Bull Street, Charleston, SC 29424

(843) 953-7609

www.cofc.edu/avery

Charleston County Public Library, with its special collections and microfilm archives, is a good source for all things Lowcountry. 68 Calhoun Street, Charleston, SC 29401

(843) 805-6980

www.ccpl.org

The **Gullah O'oman Shop and Museum** offers displays and educational talks about the Gullah language and traditions. The shop sells handmade quilts, clothing, sweetgrass baskets, toys, and more. 421 Petigru Drive, Pawleys Island, SC 29585

(843) 235-0747

Gullah Flea Market

103 William Hilton Parkway, Hilton Head Island, SC 29926

(843) 681-7374

Penn School (now Penn Center) on St. Helena Island, taken circa 1939. Courtesy of the South Caroliniana Library, USC.

The Penn Center, along with its **York W. Bailey Museum,** sits on fifty acres and chronicles the history and culture of the Gullah. It has the largest collection of papers, documents, photographs, and recordings about Gullahs (open to the public by appointment only). Penn Center has been a National Historic Landmark since 1974.

Originally used as a school for freed slaves, the center was established in 1862 by Laura Towne, who was an abolitionist and Unitarian. It later served as a center of reform. Martin Luther King Jr. planned his famous March on Washington there in 1963.

The museum opened in 1971 to preserve Sea Island and Lowcountry African American heritage. Cultural programs and lectures are offered (such as the Gullah Studies Summer Institute), and dorm rooms and cottages are available. The gift shop has many specialty items, including sweetwater baskets, handmade quilts, and books on the Gullahs. Martin Luther King Drive, St. Helena Island. (843) 838-8560 or 2432. www.penncenter.com

About St. Helena Island
(from the book *Coastal South Carolina: Welcome to the Lowcountry*)

St. Helena Island has a grim, complex history. It was the first attempt at a New World settlement, an Indian burial mound, the origin of slave trading, and an asylum for those seeking religious freedom.

The first white man to lay claim to this island was Francisco Gordillo, an explorer who had been sent by seven wealthy Spaniards. He came ashore here on August 18, 1520, which was St. Helen's Day. In honor of that saint, Gordillo not only proclaimed the land for Spain, but called it Santa Elena (St. Helen). Gordillo and his expedition were warmly greeted by the Indians, who brought them ashore, showed them around, and shared food with them. Gordillo reciprocated by inviting the natives out to his ships, but instead of providing them with a good meal and trinkets, he set sail with his first group of slaves. The Indians never made it to Hispaniola, where they were to work the gold mines, because the ships were lost at sea.

Huguenots arrived at St. Helena hoping to escape religious persecution. Instead, most were killed by Spanish Catholics. The original settlers died of famine or fever or fled. This island served as an outpost for the Spanish until 1587. Franciscan friars set up missions all along the coast, from Florida to Santa Elena. However, the priests were heavily restricted by the Spanish government. Spain was only interested in colonizing natives, particularly in regard to education and agriculture.

The next significant impact came in 1663 when English explorer William Hilton arrived and claimed the area for England. Once again, the Indians welcomed the white man and shared their land and resources. The first English settler to call St. Helena Island home was Thomas Nairn. He had a plantation on the south side of the island in 1698. More and more land grants were given as colonists arrived.

By 1707, the Indians were ordered to confine themselves to a reservation that extended from the upper end of the Combahee River to the Savannah River. Most of the Indians on the islands were Yemasees who had been helpful to the English, so part of St. Helena (Polawana Island) was set aside as a small reservation for them.

The first white child was born on St. Helena in 1700. Because of the remoteness of the island, most planters also maintained residences in Beaufort or Charleston. Because there were no stores or doctors on the island, some plantation owners chose not to live on the island at all and left daily management to their overseers. The most direct route to St. Helena was across Lady's Island and the only way to get there was by boat. A rudimentary bridge linking these two islands was built in 1744.

Most islanders were Episcopalians who attended St. Helena Episcopal Church in Beaufort. By 1740, there was a chapel on the island. By the nineteenth century, Beaufort area islands, including St. Helena, made planters wealthy. In 1850, St. Helena cultivated more than 1 million pounds of Sea Island cotton. Population swelled. Several service organizations, such as the St. Helena Agricultural Society and St. Helena Mounted Riflemen, were formed.

During the Civil War, planters and their families left St. Helena and other area islands for safer places. The slaves who remained either went into hiding or continued their duties until food rations ran out. Rumors abounded across the state that the Union Army occupied certain South Carolina sea islands and anyone seeking refuge would be protected. Many people, especially women and children, died of exposure, starvation, or drowning before they made it to the islands. Those who survived the journey were sent to Edisto Island or St. Helena Island. Whatever the military didn't use or consume, the refugees were allowed to have.

After the war, many plantations were sold to Northerners, who used the land for hunting. Marshtackies, a nickname given to the tough, little horses with extremely curly hair, freely roamed St. Helena. When it was populated, the horses were used to pull wagons over dirt roads on the island.

Teachers, preachers, and missionaries arrived at St. Helena

The bridge joining St. Helena Island to the mainland opened in 1927. Courtesy of the South Caroliniana Library, USC.

and founded Penn School in 1862 for freed island slaves. Youths were taught important skills such as reading, writing, farming, construction, and cooking. A public school opened on the island in the late 1940s, and in 1953, Penn School became Penn Center. The former school became a center for reform, tackling all kinds of issues that impacted blacks. Dr. Martin Luther King Jr. came to Penn Center in 1963 to meet with other black leaders and plan his march on Washington.

St. Helena is one of the largest sea islands in the state. Today, the 15-mile long and 8-mile wide island is mainly agricultural. It grows more tomatoes than any other place in South Carolina. Frogmore is a community on St. Helena Island. It was made famous by the legendary root doctor, Dr. Buzzard.

The **Rice Museum** is a great place to learn more about the area's rice history. It is located inside the Old Market Building in the historic district. 633 Front Street, Georgetown, SC 29442

(843) 546-7423

www.ricemuseum.org

Slave Relic Museum

208 Carn Street, Walterboro, SC 29488

(843) 549-9130

www.slaverelics.org

Life on the Plantation

The Lowcountry was ideal for growing Sea Island cotton, indigo, and rice. After the American Revolution, indigo plantations gave way to rice production. By 1840, Georgetown County produced almost half of all the rice grown in America and exported more rice than any other port in the world. Plantation owners and their families had to leave the plantations in the hands of their slaves for the summer months due to the great risk of the deadly "fever" (to which the slaves seemed less susceptible). They didn't know at that time that the rice fields and Lowcountry humidity brought mosquitoes carrying malaria. The Civil War was the beginning of the end of rice production in Georgetown.

South Carolina Artisans Center is the state's official folk art center and offers handmade products from close to 250 artists across the state. The eight-room Victorian cottage is the perfect backdrop for live performances, craft demonstrations, special events, and showcasing talented artists. 334 Wichman Street, Walterboro, SC 29488

(843) 549-0011

www.scartisanscenter.com

Note: There are many galleries in the Lowcountry that have large collections of African American art. Check with the local tourism office for a current list.

The **South Carolina Historical Society** has impressive collection of historical materials. Free for members but there is a research fee for non-members.100 Meeting Street, Charleston, SC 29401

(843) 723-8584

www.southcarolinahistoricalsociety.org

UltimateGullah.com is a good site for learning about and buying Gullah products. They sell sweetgrass baskets, art, spices, healing tonics, books, dolls, and more. P.O. Box 2098, Conway, SC 29528

(843) 488-4885

About Sweetgrass Baskets

Part of the Gullah heritage is making sweetgrass baskets by hand. Gullah basket weaving originated in Africa and was brought to America by slaves. The technique for making the coiled baskets is vastly different from that of the European weave. Baskets made of sweetgrass were in big demand on the plantations for storage of breads, fruits, clothes, household items, crops, and for selling at market. Sweetgrass baskets sell at Lowcountry roadside stands along Highway 17 or in Charleston's City Market for high prices. Visitors are often surprised at the cost for these baskets, but should remember that it takes twelve to sixteen hours to create a simple fruit basket!

Events

The following events usually include food, arts and crafts, storytelling, and musical performances. Check with the local tourism offices for more information.

Annual Penn Center Heritage Days Celebration on St. Helena Island offers an old-fashioned prayer service, Gullah cuisine, historians, artists, storytelling, basket-weaving demonstrations, and performances. (second weekend of November)

Gullah Festival in Beaufort offers events throughout the area, including tours, music, Gullah handicrafts, and food. (weekend before Memorial Day, May)

Gullah Festival highlights the heritage of Gullah people through music, food, and arts and crafts. Courtesy of the Beaufort Regional Chamber of Commerce.

Hallelujah!

The Hallelujah Singers was formed in 1990 by Marlena Smalls to showcase Gullah music and to educate others about the Gullah culture. They have made many media appearances, including the *Today* show, *Good Morning America*, and the movie *Forrest Gump*. The group has won many awards and honors. Some of their albums include: *Gullah—Songs of Hope, Faith & Freedom; Carry Me Home;* and *Joy—A Gullah Christmas.*

Gullah Rice Festival is part of Treasure of the Tidelands, which takes place on Pawleys Island, Litchfield, and Georgetown. The celebration features the Indigo Choral Society, special programs and storytelling, a fish fry, parade, and more. (May)

Hallelujah Singers' Summer Concert on Hilton Head Island (August)

Island Heritage Festival on James Island and Folly Beach features a Taste of Gullah, Children's Cultural Literacy Festival, a sunset Gullah cruise, and more. (June)

The MOJA Arts Festival in Charleston showcases literary events, dance performances, and music. (September & October)

Native Island Gullah Celebration on Hilton Head has activities throughout the month, such as a film festival, art show, banquet, and more. (February)

Tours
Contact these companies for specific itineraries and costs.

Gullah Heritage Trail Tours takes participants to the old one-room schoolhouse, the First Freedom Village Historic Marker, Gullah family compounds, and more.
>   Hilton Head Island, SC
>   (843) 681-7066
>   www.gullaheritage.com

Gullah-N-Geechie Mahn Tours features the Brick Baptist Church (built in 1855, oldest church on the island), Praise House, and Penn Center. P.O. Box 7516, St. Helena Island, SC 29920
>   (843) 838-7516
>   www.gullahngeechietours.net

Gullah Tours goes to the Old Slave Mart, slave quarters, the Whipping House, Catfish Row, and more.

(843) 763-7551

www.gullahtours.com

(Charleston and Beaufort areas)

Old Point and Gullah Island Tour

Cassettes and CDs detailing a driving tour of Old Point and the Gullah islands can be found at the Beaufort Chamber of Commerce Visitor Center. 2001 Boundary Street, Beaufort, SC 29902

(843) 525-8500

www.beaufortsc.org

Rev.'s Gullah Island Tour features the Chapel of Ease and Penn Center. P.O. Box 570, St. Helena Island, SC 29920

(843) 838-3185

Tours de Sandy Island "A Geechee Gullah Tour" takes visitors to the boat accessible–only Sandy Island (Georgetown County) to see historic sites such as the School Boat, cemetery, Fire House, and New Bethel Missionary Baptist Church (1880).

(843) 408-7187

www.toursdesandyisland.com

(Sandy Island, Georgetown County)

Ultimate Gullah Tours (SC and GA) offer several different tours throughout the lower Grand Strand and Lowcountry.
1601 Horry St., Conway, SC 29527
(843) 488-4885
www.ultimategullah.com

This is the dock and school boat used by Sandy Island residents. Photo by Terrance Zepke.

Learning Activities

Here are some ideas for those who want to further explore Gullah culture.

1. Make a collage representing the history of the Gullahs from their departure from West Africa to today. Examples: their journey to America, plantations, sweetgrass baskets, food, traditions, beliefs, praise houses, etc.

2. Learn more about sweetgrass baskets. For example, did you know they can sell for hundreds of dollars? Or that it is usually illegal to harvest sweetgrass unless you are a Gullah (and even then there are restrictions)? Research where sweetgrass can be found. Find out how long it takes to make a basket. How are they made? What were they originally used for?

3. What is a boo hag? Write a brief description. Name three things that should stop a boo hag.

4. Write a tale about and draw a sketch of a boo hag.

5. Put together a presentation about Lowcountry voodoo. Whether it is written or oral, it should answer these questions: What is Lowcountry voodoo? Who practices it? How does it work? Is it still practiced today?

6. Organize and perform a skit about a root doctor, haint, or boo hag. If you have trouble coming up with ideas, base it on one of the tales from this book, such as "The Boo Hag Bride" or "Why You Shouldn't Mess with Voodoo."

7. Plan an authentic Gullah meal. Be sure to explain either verbally or with a placard what each dish represents. Examples: Benne seed wafers (these cookies represent good luck), Lowcountry red rice, jambalaya, Hoppin' John, Frogmore stew, she crab soup, Carolina hobo bread, Gullah green beans, sweet potato pie, cornbread or cornbread casserole, biscuits, and gumbo. Store-bought items can be used instead of cooking from scratch. Benne seed cookies are sold all over Charleston.

8. Write your own Gullah folktale. The Gullah brought many stories with them from Africa and, as they shared the stories over the years, adapted them to fit their experiences in America. The most popular character in Gullah folklore is an animal called Brer Rabbit. There are many books on this subject, but one of my favorites is Joel Chandler Harris' *Classic Tales of Brer Rabbit*. The children's stories in this collection are moral teachings about a trickster character who uses his wits to get the better of others. The rabbit is believed to represent the slave who outwits his owner by using extreme measures when times call for it. A classic American plantation folktale is "Tar Baby and Brer Rabbit."

9. Research how to make a simple quilt and then design a pattern (you don't have to actually make the quilt). When creating your pattern, remember that quilts tell stories, so your design should say something, maybe about you or your family or your favorite place or tale. The art of quilt-making has been passed down among Gullahs.

10. What's happening with the Gullahs today? How many live in the U.S., and in what parts of the country do they mainly live? What are we doing to preserve their culture and folklore? Is it enough, or should we be doing more?

11. Go to one of the places or festivals (or take a tour) discussed earlier in this chapter to learn more about Gullah music, food, history, language, handicrafts, historical sites, and traditions/beliefs.

References

Adams, Dennis, and Hillary Barnwell. "The Gullah Language and Sea Island Culture, Part II: Sea Island Culture." Beaufort County Library. www.co.beaufort.sc.us/BFTLIB/gullah2.htm

Barnwell, Hillary (Beaufort County Library Assistant Director). "Vignettes of African-American History." Paper presented at the Lowcountry Traditions and Transitions Symposium, University of South Carolina, in Beaufort, SC, October 4, 1997. © 1997

Bennett, John. *The Doctor to the Dead: Grotesque Legends and Folk Tales of Old Charleston.* Columbia: University of South Carolina Press, 1995. First published in 1943 by Rinehart & Co.

Branch, Muriel Miller. *The Water Brought Us: The Story of the Gullah-Speaking People.* New York: Cobblehill Books/Dutton, 1995.

Christensen, A.M.H. *Afro-American Folklore: Told Round Cabin Fires on the Sea Islands of South Carolina.* Boston: J.G. Cupples Co., 1892.

Coming Through: Voices of a South Carolina Gullah Community from WPA Oral Histories. Collected by Genevieve W. Chandler; edited by Kincaid Mills, Genevieve C. Peterkin, and Aaron McCollough. Columbia, SC: University of South Carolina Press, 2008.

Dabbs, Edith M. *Sea Island Diary: A History of St. Helena Island.* Spartanburg, SC: The Reprint Company, 1983.

Daise, Ronald. "Early One Mornin', Death Come Creepin' in M'Room!" in *Reminiscences of Sea Island Heritage: Legacy of Freedmen on St. Helena Island.* Sandlapper Publishing, 1986.

Davis, Rod. *American Voudou: Journey into a Hidden World.* Denton, TX: University of North Texas Press, 1999.

Dunkelman, Mark H. "A Bold Break for Freedom." *American History Illustrated,* December 1999.

Glanton, Dahleen. "Gullah Culture in Danger of Fading Away." Reprinted in *Susquehanna Life,* Fall 2008 (originally published in the *Chicago Tribune,* 2001). http://www.susquehannalife. com/index.php?page=gullah-culture

Gonzales, Ambrose E. *The Black Border: Gullah Stories of the Carolina Coast.* Columbia: The State Co., 1922.

Graydon, Nell S. *Tales of Edisto.* Atlanta: R.L. Bryan Company, 1955.

Guthrie, Patricia. "Sea Islanders"in Volume II of *American Immigrant Cultures: Builders of a Nation.* Macmillan Reference, 1997.

Hare, Mildred and Chalmers S. Murray. "Hags," in *South Carolina Folk Tales: Stories of Animals and Supernatural Beings.* Compiled by Workers of the Writer's Program of the Work Projects

Administration in the State of South Carolina. Columbia: University of South Carolina Press, 1941.

Haskins, Jim. *Voodoo & Hoodoo: The Crafts as Revealed by Traditional Practitioners.* Scarborough House, 1978.

Jaquith, Priscilla, and Ed Young, illus. *Bo Rabbit Smart for True: Folktales from the Gullah.* New York: Philomel Books, 1981.

Jones, Charles Colcock, Jr. *Gullah Folktales from the Georgia Coast.* Athens, GA: University of Georgia Press, 2000.

Jones-Jackson, Patricia. *When Roots Die: Endangered Traditions on the Sea Islands.* Athens: University of Georgia Press, 1987.

Jordan, Laylon Wayne, and Elizabeth H. Stringfellow. *A Place called St. John's: The Story of John's, Edisto, Wadmalaw, Kiawah, and Seabrook Islands of South Carolina.* Spartanburg, SC: The Reprint Company, 1998.

Lockley, Timothy James, ed. *Maroon Communities in South Carolina.* Columbia, SC: University of South Carolina Press, 2008.

Long, Carolyn Morrow Long. *A New Orleans Voudou Priestess: The Legend and Reality of Marie Laveau.* Gainesville: University Press of Florida, 2006.

Malbrough, Ray T. *Charms, Spells & Formulas: for the Making and Use of Gris-Gris, Herb Candles, Doll Magick, Incenses, Oils and Powders—To Gain Love, Protection, Prosperity, Luck, and Prophetic Dreams.* Woodbury, MN: Llewellyn Publications, 1986.

Malbrough, Ray T. *The Magical Power of the Saints: Evocation and Candle Rituals*. Woodbury, MN: Llewellyn Publications, 2002.

Mitchell, Allen. *Wadmalaw Island: Leaving Traditional Roots Behind.* Roslyn, PA: Boar Hog Tree Press, 1996.

Mitchell, Faith. *Hoodoo Medicine: Gullah Herbal Remedies*. Rev. ed. Columbia, SC: Summerhouse Press, 1999.

Mitchell, Faith. *Hoodoo Medicine: Sea Island Herbal Remedies.* Berkeley, CA: Reed, Cannon, and Johnson Co., 1978.

Murray, Chalmers S. "Boo-Hags." In *South Carolina Folk Tales: Stories of Animals and Supernatural Beings*, compiled by Workers of the Writer's Program of the Work Projects Administration in the State of South Carolina. Columbia: University of South Carolina Press, 1941.

Parsons, Elsie Clews. *Folklore of the Sea Islands, South Carolina.* Cambridge, MA: American Folklore Society, 1923.

Pinckney, Roger. *Blue Roots: African-American Folk Magic of the Gullah People*. St. Paul, MN: Llewellyn Publications, 1998.

Robinson, Sallie Ann. *Cooking the Gullah Way, Morning, Noon, and Night*. Chapel Hill: University of North Carolina Press, 2007.

Robinson, Sallie Ann. *Gullah Home Cooking the Daufuskie Way: Smokin' Joe Butter Beans, Ol' 'Fuskie Fried Crab Rice, Sticky-Bush Blackberry Dumpling, and Other Sea Island Favorites.* Chapel Hill: University of North Carolina Press, 2003.

Rosengarten, Dale. *Row upon Row: Sea Grass Baskets of the South Carolina Lowcountry.* Distributed for the McKissick Museum. Columbia: University of South Carolina Press, 1986.

Rosengarten, Dale. "Spirits of Our Ancestors: Basket Traditions in the Carolinas." In *The Crucible of Carolina: Essays in the Development of Gullah Language and Culture,* edited by Michael Montgomery. Athens: University of Georgia Press, 1994.

Tallant, Robert. *Voodoo in New Orleans.* New Orleans: Pelican Publishing Company, 1983.

Teish, Luisah. *Jambalaya: The Natural Woman's Book of Personal Charms and Practical Rituals.* HarperOne, 1988.

The Island Packet Online. "Gullah Heritage: The language of the Sea Islands [Special to The Packet]." *The Island Packet,* 2000. www.islandpacket.com/man/gullah/language.html

Zepke, Terrance. *Coastal South Carolina: Welcome to the Lowcountry.* Sarasota, FL: Pineapple Press, 2006.

Zepke, Terrance. *Ghosts of the Carolina Coasts: Haunted Lighthouses, Plantations, and Other Historic Sites.* Sarasota, FL: Pineapple Press, 1999.

Index

Lowcountry Voodoo

Middleton, Frank (*see* Rumpetty
	Dick)
mojo bags, 28, 86
money, 3, 11, 16, 35, 79, 94, 96,
	97, 99, 106
	charms, 30, 32, 35, 65, 86
Mt. Pleasant, 124
Nairn, Thomas, 128
New Orleans, 1, 102, 114
New Orleans Pharmacy Museum,
	102
Nigeria, 1, 106
New York, 103, 112
Nuwaubian Pyramids, 107

Olokun Festival, 108
Ouanga bags, 28
Oyotunji, Kingdom of, 105–9

Pawleys Island, 126, 135
Penn Center, 126, 131, 134
Penn School, 131
plateyes, 19, 45, 59–63, 64, 71, 72,
	114
Polawana Island, 128
Pope, Jorico, 89
Porcher, Francis, 86
Powell, George, 73–75
praise houses, 4, 136
presider, 4, 114

Queen Elizabeth root, 31, 33

Republic of Benin, 106
Revolutionary War (*see* American
	Revolution)
rice, 17, 19, 20, 21, 24, 25, 81, 124,
	131, 132, 135
Rice Museum, 131
Ring Shout ritual, 4
rituals, 1–5, 9, 27–35, 36–41,
	42–43, 55, 69, 77, 86, 108,
	111, 114
Robinson, Stephaney (*see* Dr.
	Buzzard)
root doctor, 2, 4, 6, 19, 64, 77–85,
	86–88, 89, 90, 92, 94, 101,
	112, 113, 114
roots, 2, 3, 6, 18, 28, 31, 33, 81, 83,
	84, 86–87, 111, 113
Rumpetty Dick, 89–91

Sanders, Berry, 62–63
Sandy Island, 137, 138
Santa Elena, 127, 128
Santería, 1, 107, 115
saraka, 12
Savannah, 1, 6, 31, 97
Sea Island cotton, 24, 125, 129, 132
seekers, 4
Senegal, 1
Sheldon (South Carolina), 105, 109
Slave Relic Museum, 131
sorcerers, 4, 77, 84
sorcery, 1, 3, 84

150

South Carolina Artisans Center,
124, 132
South Carolina Historical Society,
133
spells, 2, 4, 6, 27–43, 67, 69, 87,
103,
Stabler, Edward, 101–2

Stabler-Leadbeater Apothecary
Museum, 101–2
St. Helena Episcopal Church, 129
St. Helena Island, 71, 77, 79, 82,
85, 119, 121, 126, 127–31,
134, 136, 137
St. Simons, 121
Southern buttermilk biscuits, 23
Southern collard greens, 18
Southern cornbread, 22
sweetgrass baskets, 126, 133

Trinity United Methodist Church,
74

UltimateGullah.com, 133
U.S. War Department, 82

vodou, 1, 2, 107, 114
vodoun, 1, 2
voodoo, 1–7, 30, 45, 65, 69, 81,
102, 106, 107, 112
voodoo dolls, 7, 27, 36-41
Voodoo Village (*see* Kingdom of
Oyotunji)

Walterboro (South Carolina), 124,
131, 132
Warren, "Hot-Bread-Cut" Jack, 89
West Africa, 1–2, 19, 21, 24, 77,
116, 121
white flight, 21, 24
Wilmington (North Carolina), 123
witch doctors, 4, 6, 19, 45, 77–85,
86–88, 89–91, 92, 112
witches, 46–58, 68–70, 75, 112,
114
World War II, 82, 121

Yemassee, 109, 128
Yemoja, 108
Yoruba, 105–9

Here are some other books from Pineapple Press on related topics. For a complete catalog, visit our website at www.pineapplepress.com. Or write to Pineapple Press, P.O. Box 3889, Sarasota, Florida 34230-3889, or call (800) 746-3275. For more information on Terrance Zepke's books and future projects, see www.terrancezepke.com.

Also by Terrance Zepke

Best Ghost Tales of North Carolina, Second Edition, and *Best Ghost Tales of South Carolina.* The actors of the Carolinas' past linger among the living in these thrilling collections of ghost tales. Use Zepke's tips to conduct your own ghost hunt.

Ghosts of the Carolina Coasts. Taken from real-life occurrences and Carolina Lowcountry lore, these thirty-two spine-tingling ghost stories take place in prominent historic structures of the region.

Ghosts and Legends of the Carolina Coasts. More spine-chilling tales and fascinating legends from the coastal regions of North and South Carolina.

Ghosts of Savannah. One of the most haunted cities in America, Savannah has its share of ghosts. Find out why an exorcism had to be conducted at the Hampton-Lillibridge House, about the ghost cat at the Davenport House, and about the rowdy spirits at Pirate's House who can be heard demanding more to drink.

Pirates of the Carolinas, Second Edition. Thirteen of the most fascinating buccaneers in the history of piracy, including Henry Avery, Blackbeard, Anne Bonny, Captain Kidd, Calico Jack, and Stede Bonnet.

Lighthouses of the Carolinas. Eighteen lighthouses aid mariners traveling the coasts of North and South Carolina. Here is the story of each, from origin to current status, along with visiting information and photographs. Revised to include up-to-date information on the long-awaited and much-debated Cape Hatteras Lighthouse move, plus websites for area visitors' centers and tourist bureaus. Over 100 photos.

Coastal North Carolina. Terrance Zepke visits the Outer Banks and the Upper and Lower Coasts to bring you the history and heritage of coastal communities, main sites and attractions, sports and outdoor activities, lore and traditions, and even fun ways to test your knowledge of this unique region. Over 50 photos.

Coastal South Carolina. From Myrtle Beach to Beaufort, South Carolina's Lowcountry is steeped in history and full of charm, and author Terrance Zepke makes sure you don't miss any of it. A must-have for vacationers, day-trippers, armchair travelers, and people looking to relocate to the area.

Ghosts of the Carolinas for Kids. Features eighteen stories about spirits, monsters, and even phantom pirates. Ages 8–12.

Pirates of the Carolinas for Kids. The Carolinas had more than their share of pirates, including Calico Jack, Billy Lewis, Long Ben Avery, and two women, Anne Bonny and Mary Read. Ages 9 and up.

Lighthouses of the Carolinas for Kids. The history of and facts about lighthouses along the Carolina coasts. Includes color photos and illustrations, ghost stories, and a quiz. Ages 9 and up.

Other books on the Carolinas and the South

The Legend of the Lowcountry Liar and Other Tales of a Tall Order by Brian McCréight. Thirteen tall tales told by Jim Aisle, the Lowcountry Liar himself, whose homespun yarns weave fact and fiction like Gullah women make sweetgrass baskets.

Lighthouse Ghosts and Carolina Coastal Legends by Norma Elizabeth and Bruce Roberts. From the Graveyard of the Atlantic to beautiful Hilton Head Island, lighthouse legends abound. Dedicated keepers haunt this fabled coast, remaining on duty long after they've passed on.

Ghosts of the Georgia Coast by Don Farrant. Visit crumbling slave cabins, grand mansions and plantation homes, ancient forts, and Indian hideouts to find restless souls, skin-walkers, and protective spirits.

Georgia's Lighthouses and Historic Coastal Sites by Kevin McCarthy. Each lighthouse, fort, historic home, plantation, and church of Georgia's coast is illustrated with a full-color painting by artist William Trotter.